Her son was on his hands and knees on his hospital bed, watching for the first glimpse of his hero

Sierra let Tucker go in first, love overwhelming her at the happiness chasing across her son's pale face.

"Tucker!" Owen beamed up at his hero. "You came. You're really here and everything."

"Sure I am, buddy."

If her son's eyes got any bigger, they would roll right out of his head.

"Mom, it's Tucker Granger! We saw him on TV when he showed that bull who was boss and set the new record. I saw. He's the best."

Tucker's warm chuckle rang with good humor and not self-importance as she was expecting. "Hold on there, little cowboy, I just had a good day. You didn't see me a month later getting thrown off a bronc five seconds in and breaking half the bones in my body."

That was exactly why she couldn't fall for a man like Tucker.

Books by Jillian Hart

Love Inspired

*A Soldier for Christmas
*Precious Blessings
*Every Kind of Heaven
*Everyday Blessings
*A McKaslin Homecoming
A Holiday to Remember
*Her Wedding Wish
*Her Perfect Man
Homefront Holiday
*A Soldier for Keeps
*Blind-Date Bride
**The Soldier's Holiday Vow
**The Rancher's Promise
Klondike Hero
**His Holiday Bride
**His Country Girl

Love Inspired Historical

*Homespun Bride
*High Country Bride
In a Mother's Arms
  "Finally a Family"
†Gingham Bride
†Patchwork Bride

*The McKaslin Clan
**The Granger Family Ranch
†Buttons & Bobbins

JILLIAN HART

grew up on her family's homestead, where she helped raise cattle, rode horses and scribbled stories in her spare time. After earning her English degree from Whitman College, she worked in travel and advertising before selling her first novel. When Jillian isn't working on her next story, she can be found puttering in her rose garden, curled up with a good book or spending quiet evenings at home with her family.

JILLIAN HART

HIS COUNTRY GIRL

Steeple
Hill®

Published by Steeple Hill Books™

STEEPLE HILL BOOKS

Steeple
Hill®

Recycling programs
for this product may
not exist in your area.

ISBN-13: 978-0-373-18032-5

HIS COUNTRY GIRL

www.SteepleHill.com

Printed in U.S.A.

Direct my steps by Your word.
—*Psalms* 119:133

Chapter One

Denver's January cold had crept into her bones. Sierra Baker shivered, rescued her hand-knit cardigan from the back of the uncomfortable black chair in the hospital's waiting area and watched a nurse pad down the hall to the busy nurse's station. No sign of Tucker Granger yet. She wrapped her arms around her middle for comfort and thought of her six-year-old son in his room. He was waiting for a visit from the rodeo rider he'd specifically requested of the children's wishing charity.

And the man was late. Her stomach had twisted into such a tight knot she could hardly breathe. Minutes had ticked by, minutes which had felt like hours, and anxiety was about to gobble her up.

Remember, God is in charge. That thought comforted her enough that she could settle back into her chair and gather up her knitting. The needles felt cool against her fingertips as she wrapped a strand of soft blue wool around the needle and began a row. It gave her something to focus on other than the fact her son was facing surgery bright and early in the morning.

He's going to be all right. She had to believe that. Her town pastor had encouraged her to be positive. Owen was in God's hands. She had to trust that this surgery to cure his heart problem would go flawlessly and he would be well.

"Sierra Baker. Is that you?" A man's amused baritone boomed across the waiting room, at odds with the somber, hushed tones around her.

Why did it have to be Tucker Granger? Of all the rodeo champions in the West, why did Owen want him? She and Tucker were from the same hometown. They'd gone through school together. She did not like him or the way he bounded into sight with his signature megawatt grin. That grin could make every eligible woman in a five-mile radius dream, but not her. He might be one of the most well-known bronc riders in three states, but her heart rate remained unaffected.

She folded up her knitting and rose from the chair. "You're late."

"Fifteen minutes, tops." Tardiness didn't concern him, obviously. He simply flashed his double dimples, the ones that could make him outshine a movie star, and the cane he walked with became hardly noticeable. "It was a battle getting from the airport. The planes are grounded. God was watching out for us because my flight was the last to land."

"I'm grateful, for Owen's sake." She didn't want Tucker to think she was one of the poor, perhaps misguided women who thought a man chasing notoriety and a carefree lifestyle was attractive. Not just a carefree lifestyle, she corrected, glancing at the cane he leaned on, but a dangerous one. The whole town back home had been buzzing with concern when he'd been injured months ago at a competition.

Why did his eyes flash amusement, as if he were laughing at her? That was another thing she didn't want to like about the man—his perpetual good humor.

"How is the little tyke doing?" He turned serious and jammed his free fist into his leather jacket. Snow dusted the brim of his hat and the wide expanse of his linebacker shoulders. His deep, lapis-blue eyes radiated a genuine concern, reminding her of the boy she used to know when they'd been in the same third grade class. The boy who had given her his lunch when bullies on the playground had taken hers. She'd almost forgotten that boy.

"Owen is doing as well as can be expected." She took a step toward the nurse's station. "That's why I was waiting out here. I want to talk to you before you see him."

"Sure. What's up?" He shifted the strap of a backpack on his shoulder.

A child's backpack, she realized. One with the rodeo association's logo and a bucking horse and rider printed on it. Thoughtful of him to bring a gift. She slowed her pace, so they wouldn't arrive at Owen's room too quickly.

"His surgery is in the morning. I don't know if Janelle told you."

"Sure she did. She said Owen's a pretty sick little boy right now."

"Yes, but he's going to get better." He had to. She set her chin, determined to stay strong. "He's fragile and we're trying not to upset him."

"That's the last thing I want to do."

"Please don't mention his father."

"You mean Ricky isn't here?"

"He couldn't be bothered." A long, painful story, one she so did not want to get into. "Owen is very sensitive about his dad's absence."

"I understand. Anything else I should know?"

"Just that he is really excited about you coming to see him."

"Hey, it's the least I can do. You've served my family how many meals at the town diner?" Kindness softened the rugged planes of his granite face. How the man could possibly get any more handsome was a complete mystery.

"More meals than I can count." She had been a waitress in the town's only diner since high school. "Your family is always so great to me. Your dad is a shamelessly big tipper."

"He's generous to a fault." Affection edged into his voice when he spoke of his father. Everyone knew Frank Granger was one of the good guys. Tucker, who looked nearly identical to his dad, had his mother's restlessness, as many in the town had said, but he didn't look restless as he fastened his honest gaze on Sierra. "Everyone in Wild Horse wants me to let you know that they are all praying for Owen. That's a lot of prayer coming this way."

"I know. I can feel it." She didn't seem as alone. Somehow it was as if all those loving prayers and well wishes wrapped around her like an invisible hug. "There's nothing like the community of a small town. I would be lost without everyone there."

"We're all anxious for you and Owen to come back home safe and sound and well again." For a happy-go-lucky man, Tucker could be steady and solid. Dark hair tumbled from beneath his hat, which he swept off as he raked the strands out of his eyes. "I'm praying for Owen, too. I was touched that he asked for me. He could have wanted a visit from an ex-president or a celebrity."

"There's no accounting for taste." The quip surprised her. She hadn't been in a light mood in many months. Tucker's chuckle rumbled through the sterile hallway like sunshine, causing a nurse and a patient in a wheelchair to turn his way and share a smile.

Owen's door was open, and the little boy was on his hands and knees on his bed watching for the first glimpse of his hero. Sierra stayed behind and let Tucker go in first, love overwhelming her at the happiness chasing across her son's pale face.

"Tucker!" Owen beamed up at his hero. His hand swiped at his dark hair falling into his big blue eyes. "You came. You're really here and everything."

"Sure I am, buddy. If I remember right, you and I have met before." The big man swept off his hat, his tone warm and friendly as he stuck out his hand. "Once at church when I was back home for Christmas and a long time ago at the diner."

"Yep. I was almost done with my chocolate milkshake when you came in. You had a big shiny belt buckle then, too." Owen slipped his small pale, bluish hand into Tucker's sunbrowned one and shook like a little man. "Is that cuz you were the champion?"

"You know it. Of course, I haven't won anything lately."

"You got thrown off a horse. That's why you've got that cane, right?" If his eyes got any bigger, they would roll right out of his head.

"Goodness, lie back, Owen." Sierra moved into the room, using her mother's tone because she was comfortable in that role. It created distance between her and Tucker as she circled entirely too close to him to reach her son's side. She plumped his pillows and patted the top one. "Come on, you need to take it easy."

"But, Mom, it's Tucker Granger! We saw him on TV when he showed that bull who was boss and set the new record. I saw. He's the best."

Tucker's warm chuckle rang with good humor and not self-importance as she'd been expecting. "Hold on there, little cowboy, I just had a good day. You didn't see me a month later get thrown off a bronc and break a bunch of bones."

"Wow!" Owen flopped against his stack of pillows, his entire attention focused on his hero. "Did it hurt lots?"

"Sure did. That's why I'm still walking with this cane. But I'm better now." Tucker Granger shrugged one big shoulder as if his injuries were no big deal. Of course, in her opinion grown men should not be trying to ride a horse that did not want to be ridden in the first place. Men like that, regardless of how impressive they seemed, were the kind who refused to grow up. She had issues with that sort of a man, since she'd regrettably married one of them.

"I hear you've got a big surgery coming up." Tucker sat on the edge of the bed, his deep blue gaze tender with concern. "Do you know I had some surgeries, too?"

"Wow. Did it hurt?"

"Not too bad, but then I did everything the doctors said to do. And I didn't have a nice mom to take care of me like you have." He kept it light, his tone easygoing, but it was impossible to hide the worry. "Look what I brought you."

"A backpack? Cool!"

"Not just any backpack. It's an official rodeo association one. I had a few buddies of mine sign it for you." He gave the pack a turn to show the dozen autographs and read each one aloud.

Okay, that was thoughtful. That had to have taken him a lot of time. But she couldn't let that influence her opinion of the man—of men like him.

Fine, so she was projecting. She could admit it. But the pain of Ricky's swift and abrupt abandonment was still raw. He'd been gone for nearly two years, and the wound made by his departure had never healed. She had talked to her pastor, turned to prayer and handed it over to the Lord. Yet the injury remained, one that haunted her.

Tucker Granger was not Ricky, she reminded herself, although her ex-husband's carefree attitude was not so different.

"Wow! A horse!" Owen had unzipped

the backpack and began pulling out treasures. The foot-high plastic sorrel horse with
matching mane and tail was beautiful.

"Not just any horse," Tucker explained.
"That's just like Jack."

"Jack's your horse!" It was good to see
Owen so happy. "I saw you win with him,
too. It was awesome!"

"Thanks, buddy." Cute kid. Tough to think
that tomorrow morning he would be undergoing open-heart surgery. He could see the
strain on the mother's face. Sierra Bolton,
Baker since her marriage. He zipped the
backpack open wider. "Go ahead and dig
in, Owen. There's more."

"More?" The little guy didn't let go of the
Jack replica. He plunged his free hand into
the depths of the bag, hauling out a rodeo
T-shirt in his size, a child's book about a
rodeo horse and several G-rated DVDs
Tucker figured the boy might like.

Last of all was a stuffed bull wearing a
T-shirt and a nose ring. Something for the
boy to cling to when the going got rough. It

couldn't be easy recovering from that kind of surgery. Since he'd spent his share of time in a hospital bed, Tucker could empathize.

As the boy exclaimed over each gift, Tucker's gaze kept drifting to the woman perched on the edge of an uncomfortable-looking chair. Sierra. He hadn't given her much thought, not even on the rare occasions he was home and his family dragged him out to dinner in town. He hardly recognized her without her apron and notepad. She'd grown tall and willowy, her girlhood imperfections polished away by time and maturity.

She was a beauty, with those big gray eyes and soft oval face framed by long locks of tumbling blond hair. It was hard not to admire the gentle slope of her nose, her wide-set eyes and delicate bone structure. Hard to believe she'd once been a wallflower hiding behind black-rimmed glasses, the kind of girl who handed her homework in early and landed on the honor roll every semester. The kind of girl who shied away from a boy like him. He figured that was the one thing that hadn't changed about her.

"Thank you, Tucker." Her gaze met his like a touch, and the shock bolted through him like lightning, leaving him a bit dazed.

"No problem." He hoped his grin didn't falter. He didn't normally have that reaction to women. In fact, he'd never had anything happen like that before.

"Thanks, Tucker!" Owen's excitement vibrated through the air. He studied one gift after the next with undisguised amazement. Even though he was on oxygen, it didn't seem to slow down his enthusiasm. "What's it like to ride real broncos?"

"I'll be happy to tell you, but that will be a long tale." Tucker took in the subtle signs Sierra Baker was trying to hide—the exhaustion bruising the delicate skin beneath her eyes, the tension furrowing her brow and the tight purse of her mouth as if she were doing her level best to keep all her fears inside.

Something told him she hadn't been

getting a whole lot of sleep and probably wouldn't get much, if any, tonight with the surgery looming. He took in her long hair falling straight and unadorned without a single pin or barrette or doodad. Her clothes looked rumpled, not wrinkled exactly, but as if they'd spent too much time in a suitcase, and they hung on her. A good size too large, he figured, judging by the hem of her sweater sleeve that hit her mid-palm and the cinch of her belt, the old notch where it used to be worn visible.

"Why don't you go and take some downtime?" He felt sympathy for her. He couldn't imagine his own mother putting any one of her children's needs above her own. Not that she had been a bad mother. She just hadn't been a good one, which was why he appreciated the quiet sacrifice of care Sierra made for her son. She sat on the edge of her seat, ready to leap up in case he needed anything. "I can handle things here. You go grab yourself a latte or a bite to eat. Maybe even a nap."

"No, I can't leave him." With a man she couldn't count on. She didn't say this but he could sense it. Her hands curled into small fists. "He might need me."

"I'm sure he will, but the truth is Owen and me, we need some quality man-time. It's a guy thing." He winked, hoping she would mistake his concern for her as something lighthearted. He couldn't let it get around that fearless Tucker Granger had a soft spot. That would destroy his hard-won tough-as-nails reputation. "No way can I discuss the secrets of my trade in front of a woman."

"Mom." Owen seemed scandalized, already anticipating that she wasn't about to step foot outside the door. "You can't stay. Tucker is going to tell me secrets."

"Why can't he tell them in front of me?" She flicked a lock of gold hair behind a slender shoulder. Chin up, she didn't look a thing like the wallflower he remembered. She didn't sound like one either. "I can keep a secret."

"Sure, but what about the code?" Tucker

let his eyes twinkle at her because he knew the effect it had on the ladies. There wasn't a single time he didn't get his way when he turned on the charm.

Not that he wanted to charm Sierra Baker. She was a divorced mom and that carried a whole lot of responsibility. Not that he didn't respect her for it, but obligation like that made him leery. After watching all that his dad had gone through in life, he'd played it safe and avoided entanglements of any kind. Life was easier without them, but lately he wasn't sure it was better.

"What code?" She squinted at him, and he would have given up half a year's pay to know what was going on in that head of hers. He couldn't begin to tell if his charm was working or—shockingly—backfiring.

"The cowboy code." He winked and pulled up his best smile. He knew the effect his dimples had. Mostly from experience and the fact that he had inherited them from his dad. Half the unmarried ladies in White Horse County back home harbored secret crushes on his father. He sure hoped the dimples worked for him half as well. "Don't you want me to share it with Owen?"

"Yeah, Mom? Don't you want him to share?" Owen was no slouch. He caught on quick. "Please?"

"I know when I'm not wanted." With a ghost of a smile, she rose from her chair and picked up her bag. Two knitting needles stuck out of the outside pocket. "I've got some phone calls to make. I won't be long."

"Take your time," Tucker urged.

"Yeah, Mom. Take your time," Owen parroted his hero. "We're sharin' secrets."

"Secrets, huh?" All it took was one look into her son's puppy dog eyes—the look he'd perfected when he'd wanted to try to charm her into having his way—and she melted like an ice cube in Phoenix. Impossible to say no to him. His eyes sparkled, and he looked better than he had in months. But what about the man standing in front of her, with his rugged good looks and come-what-may attitude?

"Can I trust you to stay with him until I get back?" She gave him her fiercest glare, the one Owen called her death-ray stare. She meant business. "That means you don't leave his side for any reason unless you ask Lisa on the other side of the curtain to watch him. Got that?"

"Sure. I'll stick to Owen like glue."

It was that dazzling smile she didn't trust and his too-good-to-believe looks. She was only going to the cafeteria, surely she could depend on him that much. Lisa, the mom of Taylor on the other side of the room, would keep an eye out. The nurses were right down the hall and it wasn't as if he were a stranger. She'd grown up in the same small town, rode the same school bus and endured his jokes and class clown antics through her entire adolescence. One thing she knew about the Granger family, they were decent people and Tucker had never caused anyone harm.

"We'll be like glue, Mom." Owen clasped his hands together, his forehead furrowed as if he was trying to will her to keep on going toward the door.

"Like two peas in a pod," Tucker assured her, his grin contagious.

The surgeon general ought to put a ban on that smile.

"Fine. You have thirty minutes." She ignored Owen's shout of joy and Tucker's wink. When she circled around him, she felt a shiver tremble through her soul like a warm wind's touch, something she'd never felt before.

Maybe she needed a soothing cup of coffee more than she thought. She set her chin, wrapped her hand around the strap of her bag and paused at the door. Longing filled her. She didn't want to leave Owen. He might need her.

"What secret are you going to tell me first?" Her son clutched the stuffed animal in one hand and the horse in the other. "Is it about riding broncos?"

"Yes it is, little buddy." Tucker, his back to her, seemed focused on the boy. He radiated a strength and kindness that she didn't want to believe in, although clearly Owen did.

Owen. Her heart warmed and her soul filled. Her son was all that mattered. She forced her shoes to carry her across the threshold and down the hall, giving her little boy the time he deserved with his hero.

Chapter Two

"What do you mean the flight is delayed?" Sierra tucked her cell phone against her shoulder and accepted the cashier's change. Then she remembered Tucker's comment about the planes being grounded at the airport. The implications hadn't registered at the time, but they did now. Her knees buckled and she slid into the nearest chair. The hospital dining room and its rows of empty tables echoed around her as she dropped her bag onto the floor. "No, it *can't* be."

"It might even be cancelled." Jeri Lynn Bolton was a sensible woman, the wife of a working rancher and mother of six kids.

Sierra's family hadn't had a lot of resources when she was growing up, and they didn't have a lot now. It was hard to hear her mom over the background noise in the airport. Jeri Lynn's voice saddened. "Don't worry, I won't leave you alone. Your dad and I talked about me driving, but with the road conditions and a blizzard in the mountains I'm not sure what kind of time I could make."

"No. I absolutely don't want you driving on dangerous roads." That made no sense at all. Her hand shook, and she set down her coffee on the table so it wouldn't spill. She had to stay calm. Focus on the problem. See there was only one solution, whether she liked it or not. "You'll fly in when you can. And if you can't, then you stay where you are. I've got everything covered here."

"I'm sure you do, dear, but you can't go through this alone."

"I'm perfectly fine." That was a lie, but she prayed the good Lord would forgive her. She worried her mom would get in the car and come anyway. "I have everything I need here. Owen has great doctors and the nurses are wonderful. We'll be fine."

"You can't wait through the surgery by yourself. I won't have it." Mom was upset. Worrying over her grandson's surgery was enough.

"Don't you worry about me, too." Sierra set her chin, firmed her voice and prayed her own fears did not show through. She needed her mother, she really did, but she was strong enough to get through this on her own. "Besides, I haven't heard from Ricky's folks. The Bakers may have already landed and be settling into their hotel room right now."

"You're just saying that to calm me down." A hint of relief. "I really want to be there with you, baby."

"I know." She bit her lip before she said anything that would reveal how much she'd been counting on her mom's support.

"It's killing your dad that he can't come."

"Someone has to stay and take care of the

animals." Her family grew mostly wheat but they had the usual collection of farm animals, which could not be left to fend for themselves. "You are not to drive under any circumstances. Do you understand me?"

"How did I raise such a bossy daughter?"

"I can't imagine." Sierra treasured the gentle trill of her mother's laughter.

"Say, did Tucker make it in? Owen will be so disappointed if he has to cancel."

"They are together right now. The two of them kicked me out of the room. I'm a girl and therefore not privy to their conversation." She managed to keep her hand steady enough to take a sip of the hot, sweet coffee.

"How cute. Owen must be on cloud nine."

"Pretty much." She took another sip, but it didn't steady her or calm the nerves rocking around in her stomach.

"Tucker comes from a fine family." It was hard to miss that lilt of meaning in her mother's voice. Jeri Lynn was an optimist.

"Honest, hardworking folk. And he's single."

"He's perpetually single." Tucker Granger married? She couldn't picture it. That was where the similarity between him and Ricky ended. Marriage had suited Ricky just fine, as he liked being waited on and tended to, until the going had gotten rough. She couldn't picture Tucker settling down long enough to put a wedding ring on a woman's finger. "His life is wandering from rodeo to rodeo. You'll have to find someone a little more stable to marry me off to."

"Then I'll keep trying." Beneath her mother's breezy quip vibrated the worry for Owen she was fighting to hide.

Sierra knew just what that was like. She'd been battling to do the same for the last six months, as Owen's health problems had gone from moderate to serious. "You'll have to try pretty hard," she quipped back. "It takes a great man to be better than no man at all."

"I don't know who quoted that saying to

you, but it's wrong. Your father isn't a great man, but he's better than nothing." She burst into giggles, maybe from stress rather than her gentle joke.

Sierra giggled, too. The tension was definitely getting to her. "Dad is a good man."

"I know. I just couldn't seem to help myself." Recovering, Jeri Lynn gave a sigh, as if she were prepared to compose herself. "Bad news. They've cancelled the flight. Unless the Bakers made it in, you're on your own, baby."

"I'm not alone, Mom. I can feel your love from here."

"That's right, and I'll keep it coming."

Silence fell, and Sierra knew what her mom was too choked up to speak. They were never alone, not really. She had never relied more on her faith than during the last few months, especially today. Tomorrow, her faith would be all she had to see her through the surgery to save her son's life.

"I'm having second thoughts, baby. I can still drive. If I leave right now—" Her mother paused as if calculating time and distance. "I should be able to make it in time."

"I said absolutely not." She couldn't stand the thought of her mom alone, driving through the night, battling ice, weariness and terrible conditions. "We already settled this. You're staying home."

"Maybe I can get your brother to come with me. We can trade off driving."

"No. Don't you see? I'm holding it together but if I have to worry about you, too, I don't think I can do it." She liked to think she was strong enough to handle everything, but it wasn't true. She bounced out of the chair, grabbed her bag and her mocha and headed for the exit. "Go home and stay with Dad. You two can call me tomorrow as many times as you want. We can be together that way."

"I don't like it."

"When the storm clears, you can fly in. It might be better that way. Owen will get to spend more time with you." Her voice hardly cracked, and she was pleased. The last thing she wanted was for her mom to guess how unnerved she was. The surgeon had gone over with her the risks of anesthesia, surgery in general and everything that could go wrong with the delicate procedure.

Concentrate on the positive, she reminded herself.

"He will be just fine." No one could comfort like a mother. Jeri Lynn's voice shone with certainty and love, as if she could will everything to be all right.

Sierra breathed in as much of her mother's comfort as she could. Her sneakers squeaked on the tile floor as she wended her way to the elevators. "Owen is going to get through this surgery the way he does everything. With flying colors."

"That's right. He's one special little boy."

"By this time tomorrow, he'll be in recovery and doing well." There was nothing like a little wishful thinking to put spring in a woman's step. She punched the elevator button.

"You call if you need me, baby girl." Jeri Lynn's voice rang as warm as a hug. "Anytime. Even if it's the wee hours. You hear me?"

"I promise, Mom, but I'll be fine." She intended to be fine. She intended to handle the worry, the fear and the wait in the best way possible. The doors opened. "I'll talk to you soon, Mama."

She tucked her phone in her pocket and smiled briefly at the other occupant of the elevator car, a nervous-looking accountant-type holding a small bouquet of flowers, who did not smile back. She hit the floor button and leaned against the wall. How was Owen faring with Tucker? She warmed from the inside out picturing her little boy's excitement. He was probably still clutching the plastic horse and the stuffed bull, basking in his hero's presence.

"Hi, Sierra." Allie, one of the nurse's aides,

smiled as she hurried by. "I see Owen has a visitor. A *handsome* visitor."

One look and all women were charmed. Honestly. Sierra shook her head. "He's Owen's charity wish."

"I was wondering if he was yours." Allie waggled her brows.

"Not a chance." She rolled her eyes. She'd become far too sensible to wish, even just a little.

"Then I'm going to wish for him. Christmas is already past, but I can start on my list for next year." With a wink, Allie whisked around the corner and out of sight.

Wish? It had been a long time since she'd wished for anything for herself. Sierra skidded to a halt in the corridor, drawn by the sound of her child's voice. All her wants and prayers had gone to her son. First during the rocky year before the divorce, to protect him as much as she could from the marital unhappiness, then to helping him cope with the separation from his father, who had chosen to leave town. And then she tried to shield him from his worsening health.

All I want, Lord, she prayed as she stood mesmerized in the hall by the sight of her little boy's wide grin, *is for him to be healthy again. That's all I want. Nothing more.* All her lost dreams, the long string of work-days on her feet from dawn until dusk and the tatters of her heart were nothing by comparison.

He still held the plastic horse in one hand and hugged the stuffed bull in the curve of his other arm. He was thin. He'd lost weight, his appetite had dwindled, but his baby blues sparkled and pleasure flushed his face. He hadn't spotted her yet because his entire attention was fixed on the man telling a tale.

"And then the bull gave one final kick. I ducked." Tucker crouched as if he were missing a bull's hoof by a hair and blew out a dramatic sigh of relief. "A half inch closer, and I would have been in big trouble."

"But you weren't. You showed that bull!"

"I did, but I'm not sure who came out the winner. Me or him. He gave me a good fight. Don't know how I managed to stay on as long as I did." Tucker's baritone vibrated with laughter. "Back in the barns I paid a visit to that bull."

"You did? What happened? Did he try to kick you?" Enthralled, Owen leaned closer, squeezing the stuffed bull in the crook of his arm harder. "Is he a mean bull?"

"He's powerful. He spotted me coming and he remembered me." Sounded like a tall tale to her, but he was entertaining Owen so she didn't hold it against him. Tucker leaned closer to the boy, as if to make the story more intense. Dark hair dropped over his high forehead, and in profile the straight blade of his nose and the square cut of his jaw were impressive.

Not that she was noticing.

"His eyes got big. His nostrils flared." Tucker raised one arm, imitating the animal.

"He pawed the ground, and I heard a low, menacing growl."

"Wow. Oh, wow." Owen's eyes became impossibly bigger. "What did you do?"

"I pulled a handful of molasses treats out of my pocket like this." Tucker held out his hand, palm up. "Slayer turned his head to glare at me with one eye, then he snatched the pellets out of my hand and let me rub his poll."

"Wow. You tamed him!"

"He's a good guy. He's just very good at his job, which forces me to bring my A-game when the gate opens." Tucker was obviously good with kids. She didn't want to like him, but she couldn't find fault with him for that.

As if he had become suddenly aware of her, he glanced over his shoulder. A slow grin spread across his face, revealing those lady-killer dimples. "You managed to stay away all of twenty minutes. We agreed on thirty. I want a full half hour."

"One thing you have to learn about me, Tucker." Why was she smiling, too? "I don't make it a habit to do what a man wants. Any man. Even you."

"Duly noted." He crossed his arms over his chest, as if appraising her. "You have to go away. Owen and I have ten minutes left. All my secrets have not been revealed."

"Yeah, Mom. We're busy." Owen bounded on his knees, the rasp of his oxygen like a knife to her heart. She hated seeing him like this, but the happiness radiating from him was worth the step back she took.

"Okay, fine. I'll go away." As hard as it was to leave her son again, she would retreat to the waiting room and knit a few more rows.

"Well, now, I guess we don't want to drive you off." Tucker hooked the chair she'd been sitting in with his foot and tugged it out of the corner. "Maybe you can stay if you vow not to divulge anything you hear."

"I make no promises."

"Beware, I've been known to charm the most cantankerous and ornery of animals. It might even work on you." His wink was a step away from downright laughter.

"I'm not ornery." She was *so* not sure about this man.

"I didn't say you were, but you do look tired and I did ask you to take a break. Since you refused to listen, you might as well come put your feet up. I can always hope I bore you so much you drift off and take a nap."

"As you are completely dull and lackluster, it's likely to happen." She settled into the chair and set her bag on the floor. "Is this all right, Owen? I don't want to intrude on your guy-time."

"I guess, but we've got to talk about bull and bronc riding." Owen looked adorable, her little angel. "He's gonna teach me all about it."

"I won't interfere. Promise." She held up her cup and took a sip. Now that she could see her son was all right and happy and her separation anxiety was eased, she did feel a little more relaxed. "Go on with your tale."

"My tale? I assure you this is the bona fide truth. Cowboy's honor." Tucker laid a fist across his heart. "Slayer and I aren't friends exactly but we respect one another. He's good at what he does and I am, too. Some days I'm the victor and some days he is."

"You talk to this animal? That's how you know he respects you?" So, she was giving him a little sass. Maybe he deserved it, maybe he didn't. But any man who looked that amazing and who had enough charm to disable half the female population in six states could use a little humbling.

"Sure I do. Slayer and I have had some good conver-sations."

"You mean you *like* Slayer?" Owen seemed amazed.

"Just because he and I are adversaries in the pen doesn't mean it's personal. He's one of God's creations, too." The lilt remained in Tucker's voice but his smile disappeared. "That's one of the first things my dad taught me. You don't be unkind to an animal. God gave them life for a reason and if He cares about the smallest sparrow, then He cares about all His creatures. He's watching how you treat them. He's trusting us to do it right."

"I learned that in Sunday school." Owen nodded, seriously. "We learned about sheep and the Shepherd, too."

Fine, so the cowboy secrets weren't what she'd expected, but she liked being privy to them. She leaned back in her chair and took another sip of her drink. It was chocolaty and soothing, the room was warm and the last few weeks of little sleep and incredible worry caught up with her. Exhaustion wrapped around her like a welcome hug.

"Sounds like you're learning the right stuff." Tucker's deep voice rang low and pleasant. "The thing about Slayer is he likes putting on a show and acting tough. You can see it in his eyes. He sizes you up before a run, like he's figuring out how fast he can get you to the ground."

"But he tries to gore you." Owen sounded confused.

"Sure, he gets carried away. He doesn't have reasoning powers the way humans do, but he isn't out to hurt you. He gets all wound up and his instincts take over. You can't fault him for that."

"What about the horse that stomped you?"

Tucker's voice grew blurry, one word rumbling into the next, hard to discern. Her eyelids felt so heavy. Maybe she should close her eyes. She could listen and rest at the same time, couldn't she?

The sound of Tucker's voice murmured pleasantly, growing dimmer and dimmer until there was only silence.

"I learned to ride bulls and broncs on sheep." It was hard to miss the woman snoozing quietly, her chin tucked to her chest, sitting relaxed and slack and peaceful. She sure must be tired to drift off like that. That chair didn't even look close to comfortable. She'd been out a good twenty minutes by his count, maybe more.

"On a sheep?" Owen looked a little doubtful. "You can't ride a sheep."

"Sure, I can't now, but that was back when I was a little guy about your age." The kid seemed to be lapping up his stories, so he figured, why stop? He didn't want to disappoint the boy. And if he himself were facing heart surgery the next day, he'd want to be distracted, too. "I kept pestering my dad to ride like the rodeo, so he finally caved and borrowed a few of the neighbor's sheep. I was a mite disappointed, I tell you, when my dad brought me out to the corral all pleased as punch. He figured I'd be real excited but the truth was, I was thinking, a sheep? That's not the same as bronco riding."

"A sheep isn't a horse." Owen laughed, as if that was obvious.

"Exactly. Then my dad put me on Fluffy's back. That sheep took off like a wild thing and I slid right off. I landed on my backside in the dirt thinking that was the most fun I'd ever had." The memory had him laughing. "My dad chuckled and ambled over to me and dusted me off. He said, 'What did you think of that, son? You think that's a sissy ride now?' All I wanted was to get back on that sheep and ride him better each and every time."

"Wow." Owen's face fell and he stared hard at the bull tucked tight against his chest. With his head bowed, his cowlick stuck straight up, making him look both cute and vulnerable. "What's your daddy like?"

"My dad?" The question startled him. He shot a glance at Sierra, still asleep in the chair. He did his best not to notice what a beautiful woman she was and the pretty picture she made, there in her light pink sweater and well-worn jeans, like a snapshot to be treasured over time. Her warning popped into his head. He knew the boy wasn't bringing up the issue of his missing father, but it was implied in that question.

How did he handle it? He studied the kid for a second, taking in the downcast look and the wistful tone of his question. Couldn't hurt to talk about Dad. There wasn't a better father on this earth than Frank Granger.

"I get my animal sense from him." Tucker was surprised at the wash of memories that hit. He spent most of his adult life either on the road or keeping up his training. Riding was an art, one that required practice every day and kept him far from his childhood home. That was the way he'd wanted it, so he was hard pressed to explain the beat of longing for family, for his dad.

"Was he a rodeo rider, too?" Owen asked, head up, eyes sad.

"Nope. He is a hardworking rancher. He is a good dad. The kind that's patient and steady. He listens. He was always there taking care of Mom and us kids. He taught me to whisper to the animals."

"Whisper? You mean you can *talk* to them?"

"Sure you can. You just open your mouth and say stuff."

That bit of humor almost distracted the boy from the father discussion. Owen broke a hesitating smile and rolled his eyes. "I know that. Anybody can talk to 'em. But how do you do it in horse?"

"That's a good question. Not everyone can." The memories came quietly and as welcome as a Wyoming summer, breezing through him stirring up images of his dad kneeling down, hands out, baritone rumbling like song. Frank Granger was a big man, several inches over six feet, and he'd seemed like a giant to the six-year-old boy Tucker had once been. A gentle, powerful, able-to-do-anything father he could always lean on.

"The secret is easy." Tucker said the same words to Owen that his dad had told him.

"You put your feelings in your voice and in your hands and you leave the door to your heart wide open."

Chapter Three

Sierra blinked, staring at the man, his words resounding inside her. Maybe it was sleep clinging to the corners of her mind making things fuzzy, but had Tucker Granger truly said that? She didn't realize that a man like him—one who was always laughing, carefree and without a single tie in the world to bind him—would know anything about what lived inside the heart.

"Look who is back with us." His smile warmed his voice, and she'd never thought of a man's tone as cozy before, but his was. "Sleeping Beauty is awake."

"Sleeping Beauty. Really?" Groggy she

may be, but she wasn't *that* out of it. She shook her head. "Is there an off switch to that charm of yours? It's getting a little much."

"I'll turn it down a notch." Good humor sparkled back at her. The man dazzled, that was for sure, and it was hard not to hold it against him. "Feeling better?"

"A little." Good thing she'd kept her cup upright. It was tilting a bit but hadn't spilled. She took a sip of the lukewarm goodness to give her a moment to compose herself.

"Just in time." He rose, tossing a smile at someone behind her shoulder. "Looks like pizza is here."

"Pizza?" She hadn't ordered any. The delicious aroma of dough, red sauce and pepperoni filled the air.

"Pizza!" Owen looked beyond amazed. "Really? Pepperoni and everything?"

"You betcha, little buddy." Tucker handed over a generous tip and took charge of the boxes and container of drinks. "I can see by that big frown they forgot to clue in your mom. I had Janelle clear this with your team of docs."

"Oh boy! Goody." Owen beamed joy. "Thank you, Tucker. Thank you, thank you, thank you!"

"You're welcome. I'm partial to pizza myself." He slid the boxes on the bed. "When I'm on the road, I eat way too much of it. I'm on a health kick these days, eating well so I heal up right. I can't tell you how much I've missed this stuff."

"Me, too!" Owen squeezed the stuffed bull in a big hug. "My mom says pizza is not a food group. You're only supposed to eat food groups."

"Really? That's just plain wrong." He hauled out a cup of cola from the drink holder and handed it over to her. While he was jovial, it was easy enough to read the understanding somberness in his impossibly dreamy eyes. "Pizza has dough, so that's as good as a whole grain right there."

"No, it isn't. This is a white-flour crust," she argued, laughing, too. "There is a difference between processed flour and the real stuff."

"Sure," he said, as if he didn't believe her one bit, his dimples deepening.

She set her coffee on the floor and reached for the drink he held out to her. Her fingers curled around the cold circumference of the cup and brushed the heat of his calloused, sun-browned hand. A spark snapped down her arm like an electric shock, startling her. He didn't seem to notice, pulled away and kept on talking, but the charge kept tingling and seemed to dig into the marrow of her bones. What was that? Her imagination? Static electricity in the air?

"There's the red sauce," Tucker went on, unaware of her reaction as he flung open one of the boxes. "That's made with tomatoes or tomato paste or something like that. That counts as a vegetable. And the cheese is dairy. Pepperoni is meat, so that sounds like four food groups to me."

"Me, too!" Owen was happy to agree, seeing as how he was about to benefit from the argument. "Tucker? Which is the biggest piece?"

"Let's see." Tucker grabbed a napkin and considered the pie in front of him. "This one, do you think?"

Owen leaned forward, studying the slice his hero was lifting onto a napkin. Cheese strings stretched and broke, red sauce dripped and pepperoni grease oozed.

"Yep," the boy said with satisfaction. "That one's the best piece. Can it go to my mom?"

"Sure, buddy." What a sweet kid. Tucker held out the piece to Sierra, doing his level best not to be affected by her. It wasn't her beauty that was getting to him, but something deeper, something he admired more than he wanted to admit. "It's only right that ladies are served first. I've got pineapple and Canadian bacon in the other box if you'd rather have it."

"This is great." She didn't meet his gaze but took the napkin carefully and this time their fingers didn't touch.

He couldn't say why that was a letdown. It wasn't as if he was interested in the woman. He wasn't looking for a connection or for reasons to like her.

"Which piece for you, cowboy?" he asked the kid, who had already picked out the slice he wanted and pointed. "You're going to have to put down Jack and Slayer."

"This is Slayer? Cool." Owen seemed pleased with that, although he had a hard time putting down either toy. He debated which one to let go of first, carefully released the plastic horse and set him on the bedside table. Then he propped the stuffed bull against the pillows and tucked him beneath the covers, like a good dad would.

After handing over the slice, Tucker took one for himself. "Sierra, something tells me you're just itching to say grace."

"I'm more curious to see what you are going to say." She had the most amazing eyes, the color of rain clouds gleaming in the light of a winter's dawn. She was softer toward him and there was no mistaking the curiosity playing at the corners of her pretty mouth.

"Don't worry, I'm not short on prayers." Truth was, he was a praying man, faithful to the core. He'd been brought up that way, and living on his own had reinforced his beliefs. He bowed his head, realizing his hands were full of food so they couldn't join hands. It might have been better to pray *before* doling out the pizza. Although he was a faithful man, he wasn't a farsighted one.

"Dear Father," he began, peering through his lashes to make sure Owen was doing the same. Was it his fault that he noticed Sierra, too? She was a wholesome sight, her golden hair cascading over her shoulders, true faith poignant on her heart-shaped face. He wondered what silent prayer she sent heavenward, considering tomorrow's events. "You are so good to us with all the blessings You bestow on us and on this world. I want to thank You for bringing me here today to get better acquainted with Owen. I'm sure You know and love Owen well. He's got a big day scheduled tomorrow. We ask that You watch over him, so he can get well and run and play again. And, if it's possible, let him ride a bronco one day."

"Amen!" Owen called out with excitement. "I'd sure like that."

"Amen," he muttered, biting his bottom lip to keep from laughing, noticing that solemn note in Sierra's quieter amen.

"This is good pizza." Owen chomped away, collapsing against his pillows beside Slayer. "The best. So, when do I get a bronco ride?"

Uh-oh. He immediately felt the pull of the boy's wish and the mother's unspoken disapproval. Looked like he was in trouble again. Since all eyes were on him, he swallowed hard, took a sip of cola to wash down the bite of pizza and fashioned what he hoped was a diplomatic answer. "That would be up to your mom."

"Thanks." Sierra shook her head at him and her disapproval didn't seem as serious as before. "Thank you so much for putting that on me."

"You're entirely welcome. It was my pleasure," he quipped. "What, you don't want him to turn out like me?"

"Do you think I would?" She was laughing now, mostly because Owen was bouncing on the bed again, frail of health but hearty of spirit.

"I can ride, can't I, Mom?" Owen begged. "Tucker told me how. I can do it."

"So I heard." She took a sip of soda, buying time, her forehead crinkling a bit as she thought strategically. "We'll talk about it once we're home and you have the doctor's consent."

"That means no." Owen sighed. He slumped, too good a boy to pout at not getting his way, but his disappointment was sincere and palpable.

"That means you have to heal up first." Tucker chimed in, figuring he'd better lend Sierra a hand before he fell further into her disfavor. "That's what I'm doing. I haven't tried to ride since I got out of the hospital. I haven't even thought of riding. I've got to get this leg back to normal, then I get to deal with what comes next."

"Oh. Okay." Owen took a bite of pizza, scrunching up his face as he considered the possibilities. "I'm gonna be a cowboy one day, just like you, Tucker."

"It's my guess you'll make a better one."

"He'll be the best, whatever he does," Sierra chimed in, resolute, watching her son. Her mother's love was easy to read. It polished her; it made her radiant with an inner beauty that took his breath away.

He forgot what he'd been about to say. Words vanished on the tip of his tongue, leaving him mute. He'd never seen this side of Sierra before, never really had the chance. One thing was for certain. No other woman had ever intrigued him the way she did with her steadfast love and concern for her child. It touched him down deep, where he never let anything in.

"Do you got a trailer?" Owen's enthusiasm

broke into Tucker's thoughts, bringing him back to the conversation. The kid was already working on the crust of his pizza as he awaited the answer.

"I have an RV." Tucker realized he was holding a piece of pizza and took a bite. Swallowed. "It's home to me when I'm on the road, which is a lot."

"Did you drive it here?"

"Nope. It's parked at home in my family's garage."

"With your dad?" The boy's eagerness changed into something more, a look of longing and loss. His love for his father remained in spite of his abandonment and the years of separation.

"Yep, with my dad." Sympathy filled him. He'd gone through something similar with his mom when she'd been alive. He understood the pain of an inadequate parent. "And with my sisters, too."

"Does your dad tuck you into bed at night?" Owen wiped tomato sauce off the corners of his mouth using a napkin and boyish swipes, but there was no missing the longing in his big eyes.

"Not anymore." He could feel Sierra's gaze like a touch against the side of his face. He could feel her worry that he would upset the boy with his answer. Not going to happen. "Do you know why Dad always tucked me in when I was a little guy?"

Owen shook his head.

"Because my mom wasn't there. She decided she didn't like living on the ranch and doing all that hard work, so she skedaddled. She used to read my bedtime stories and tuck me in, but when Dad took over that was nice, too."

"Your mama left?"

"Sometimes that happens. It's sad, but you are the luckiest guy I know." Tucker wadded up his napkin, praying that he said this just right. "God must love you to have blessed you so much."

"Really?" That lit the boy up, the sorrow fading and sadness vanishing.

"He gave you the best mom in the world."

He resisted the need to look at the woman seated so near to him he could hear the slight gasp of her shock. A strange liquid warmth rolled through his chest somewhere in the vicinity of his heart, an emotion he did not want to acknowledge or to feel. "I sure didn't get a mom like that."

"She is a pretty good mom," Owen agreed, carefully considering his answer.

"Glad you agree." Tucker wanted the boy to know that what he had was more important than what he'd lost. Tucker had spent a chunk of his life figuring that out. Might as well save the boy the trouble. "Your mom stays with you no matter what. She's here with you right now, right? And she's so cool that I even let her listen to some of my cowboy secrets."

"Right." Owen slowly grinned. "And she lets me pick what's on TV."

"That's what I figured." Tucker eased off the bed, his chest tight, his comfort level shattered. He liked to keep a safe distance. He liked things easy and breezy, not weighty and serious, and most of all he didn't want any entanglements. He cared for the boy. Didn't know how it had happened, but there it was. An unspeakable pain wedged between his ribs, a sign of more emotion he did not want to feel.

"Time to go," he announced, his stay had already gone well beyond the time the charity had requested of him. So it wasn't a bad thing that he needed to get some fresh air, away from the strange tug this little boy and his mother had on him.

"Do you have to go?" Owen asked, disappointment setting in.

"Tell you what. I'll give you a call when your mom gives the go-ahead to see how you're healing up after your surgery. How's that?"

"Great. Mom, did you hear? Tucker's gonna call me. We're friends."

"I heard." Sierra's voice sounded thick with emotion, layered with feelings that did more than tug at him. He felt them—her worry for her son, her gratefulness that he was happy and her wariness of a has-been rodeo rider making promises she feared he wouldn't keep.

"Got a pen?" He snagged a napkin off the stack and waited while she dug into her purse. "I'll leave my cell number so you can get ahold of me. Let me know what a great job Owen does in surgery."

"I'll be asleep," Owen laughed.

"Sure, but you're going to be the best patient ever. The surgeon is going to be in awe at how well things go." Tucker didn't like thinking of the precious little boy undergoing something so serious. Strange and unwelcome pain bored deeper into his chest and it took hard work not to let it show. He grabbed the pen Sierra offered him, seeing the same dread reflected on her beautiful face.

"This time tomorrow," he went on, turning his attention to scrawling out numbers on the napkin, "your mom will call and tell me how fantastic you're doing and that I had better find me a good sheep because you're ready to start learning the trade."

"All right!" Owen clasped his hands together, as if overcome with joy.

Only then did Tucker realize what he'd done. He'd promised to teach the boy without clearing it first with his mom. Ouch. That was one big mistake. He stared hard at the pen and napkin in hand, knowing recrimination was about to come in one form or another. It was his experience that most mothers did not want their sons to grow up to join the rodeo.

"I'll give you a call." When Sierra spoke, there wasn't veiled anger layered beneath her quiet alto. Not even a hint of coolness or a tone of disapproval. What he heard instead made him turn toward her, surprising him like nothing could. She smiled, taking the pen and napkin from him. "It's a good thing your neighbors raise sheep. We'll know just where to look."

"Right." His throat tightened. Words tumbled straight out of his head. He felt awkward and wooden as his boots hit the tile and he grappled for his cane and his hat. He didn't know why he could see her heart, but he could. She was grateful for his offer because it gave Owen hope; it gave her hope, that there would be a lifetime of to-morrows yet to come for her and her son.

"You be sure and watch some of those movies," he told the boy. "The one with the wooden toy cowboy is my favorite. When I talk to you, I want to hear what you think."

"Sure. 'Bye, Tucker." Owen wrapped his arm around the stuffed bull and held on tight.

The picture he made, sitting frail and small in his hospital bed, tore at him.

"Thanks for having me over," he said, taking a step into the hall before he real-ized it was true. He thought he'd been doing a favor for the charity, but he'd been wrong. The favor had been for him.

Sierra was on her feet, following him into the hall. Light played in the multihued layers of her hair, golds, honeys and platinums glinted beneath the fluorescent lamps. She looked lighter than when he'd met her a few hours ago, so luminous it hurt to gaze at her.

"I can't believe everything you did for Owen today." Her fingertips landed on his forearm. "Thank you."

"My pleasure." Her touch felt like the sweetest comfort he'd ever known and he did not pull away. "You promise to call? I want to know when he's out of surgery. I've got a sheep to find."

But that wasn't what he meant and judging by the gleam of emotion pooling in her gray eyes, she knew it, too. The sheep wasn't the problem. It was his concern for the boy.

"Promise." Her lower lip trembled and she fell silent, as if she could not risk saying more. She firmed her chin and straightened her slender shoulders. So much strength for such a wisp of a woman, and seeing it made him admire her all the more.

"Goodbye, Sierra." The emotion wedged

between his ribs arrowed impossibly deeper. He forced his feet to carry him down the hall and away from the woman responsible. It had to be sympathy he felt for her because, as every woman he'd ever dated had told him, he wasn't capable of more.

Chapter Four

Sierra yawned wide, covered her mouth with her hand and hated that her brain felt full of cobwebs. She stared at her phone, wondering why her mother's cell kept going to voice mail. It was probably the storm that had blown out sometime in the night. Still, a lot of services were compromised this morning. She sat straighter in the chair, trying not to make any distracting sounds in the surgical waiting area. A handful of other people anxiously waited on the surgeries of their loved ones, too.

She dialed again, tucked her phone to her ear and sighed. She missed her mom, but it strengthened her to hear the sound of her voice on the recorded message. She waited for the beep. "Hi, Mom. I don't know where you are. The home phone isn't in service either. Owen has been in surgery for about an hour. So far, so good—at least there hasn't been any word otherwise. I'll try calling you in a little bit. I love you."

She disconnected, hating the lonely, frightening feeling creeping in around the edges of her heart. That same worried terror had haunted her the night through, keeping away all chances of real sleep. Open-heart surgery came with risks, ones she had vowed not to dwell on but they surged around her now like a tidal wave. What would she do if something went wrong? She couldn't lose him. Owen was her world, every part of her life that was good and beautiful.

Lord, please keep me on the right path here. She swallowed hard, slid her phone into the outside pocket of her purse and gathered up her knitting from the empty chair beside her. *Help me to see the positive and keep all doubt away. Help Owen's surgery to go perfectly.*

Those words made her think of Tucker Granger's visit yesterday. He'd found it so easy to be optimistic and the assurance in his rumbling baritone had been strong, strong enough to touch her now.

Footsteps came to a rest beside her. She glanced up, shocked to see the man towering above her, handsome, thoroughly masculine and invincible. Tucker Granger tossed her a strained grin, a shadow of the bright one he'd mesmerized her son with yesterday.

"Thought you could use a friend." He held out a cardboard drink container with three covered paper cups. "And if I don't qualify as a friend, then I figured bringing three different kinds of coffee might give me that status for the morning."

"It's possible, but only a temporary one."

"Awesome." He settled into the chair beside her and stowed his cane. "I've got a regular, a latte and a mocha. You get first pick."

"Definitely the mocha. Thank you." Her hands started to shake, so she let her knitting fall into her lap. Relief flooded her. "Why aren't you warm and comfortable in your hotel room?"

"I felt cooped up." He extricated a cup from the container and held it out to her, his fingers a shocking warmth against hers as she took the coffee.

"Cooped up? So you thought going out in the aftermath of a blizzard with half the city streets still unplowed would be a good alternative?"

"Absolutely. A little blizzard doesn't scare me. Besides, I've been where you are before. Years ago when my dad was shot in the chest scaring off cattle rustlers." His ease faded and he tensed up as if in memory. Pain crept into his features, giving him character, making him real to her in a way he'd never been before. He chose a cup of plain coffee and leaned back in his chair. "I'll never forget the waiting while he was in surgery. It was touch-and-go the whole time."

"I remember. That was a long time ago." She took a sip. "And your sister was shot before Christmas, wasn't she?"

"One of the dangers of cattle ranching, I suppose. The occasional well-armed cattle rustler." He stared into his cup, more somber than was comfortable. "It's been a tough winter. I was trussed up in traction in a hospital room worrying the whole time Autumn was in surgery. I felt the same sick, scared feeling when Dad was fighting for his life. Turned out she wasn't hit as bad, but we still could have lost her."

"Your poor dad, worried about the both of you." Her gray eyes filled with empathy. "It's been a rough year for your family."

"And great at the same time. My big brother's married and Autumn is engaged." He gave his cup a swish to watch the coffee swirl like a whirlpool. "I'll be walking without that cane in a few more weeks, so I can check out the neighbor's sheep."

"Tough times get us through to where we need to go." She took a dainty sip of coffee, taking her time, letting it roll across her tongue.

She was pretty this morning, although she probably wouldn't think so. Her hair was pulled back in a haphazard ponytail, thick and long and bouncing against her shoulder blades. Her face without makeup was pale but luminous with her authentic, natural beauty. Her simple T-shirt and jeans had obviously been thrown on without thought. The shirt was a little askew, which he found endearing.

Not that he had any tender feelings for her. Just making an observation.

"And where is it that you are going?" he asked.

"To a place where Owen's heart is strong and well again." She didn't hesitate. Her affecting gray eyes filled as if with a prayer. "All I want is for him to be happy."

"That's what I want for him, too." He'd never spoken truer words.

He spent most of his time thinking about himself, his job and his family, sadly in that order. He didn't mean to be self-involved. He was a single man without strings or responsibilities, so his thoughts and goals naturally turned to himself. His job was demanding. He trained long hours and his best friend was his horse. He liked things this way, but he couldn't say he was happy. He couldn't say he had what mattered in life, the way Sierra did.

"I know you must be missing your mom about now and I'm one sorry substitute, but Owen is going to pull through just fine. The surgeon is going to be amazed and all that."

"So, that's your attempt to comfort me?" She shook her head. "Pathetic."

A smile stretched his mouth and dug deep inside with a glow that spread all the way to his toes. He leaned back in the chair, stretched his legs out in front of him and took another swig of coffee. "I should at least get an A for effort. I'm a cowboy. I don't know a lot about comforting women."

"Excuses, excuses."

"True, but I'm being honest. Truth is, I'm worried about Owen, too." He wasn't comfortable saying the words, but the thought of that little guy on an operating table hit him where it hurt. "Why isn't Ricky here?"

"Owen's father is having fun." She tapped her fingers against the cup, probably thinking she was hiding her anger and pain. Her soft alto sounded brittle. "I left messages on his voice mail for almost a whole three weeks, telling him about Owen's condition and the surgery they scheduled, but nothing. He hasn't even bothered to call and see how his son is doing."

"What do the Bakers say about all this?" He knew the family Sierra had married into. Their hometown was small, and they had all grown up together. "They are good people. They can't be okay with this."

"They've been wonderful. Betty and Chip have been great in-laws to me and fantastic grandparents to Owen. They are disappointed in their son." She shrugged her slender shoulders, unaware of how vulnerable she looked. She might want to pretend otherwise but her divorce had taken a toll.

He understood, which was why he kept free and clear of entanglements. That didn't mean he couldn't appreciate what she'd been through. Long shifts at the diner, working at near minimum wage. She had it tough. He didn't have to ask if Ricky was paying his child support payments.

"The Bakers were supposed to be here, too. I haven't heard from them either." She swallowed hard, boldly set her chin and met his gaze. "The storm has thrown a wrench into everything. I'm praying they are safe. I know they wanted to be here for Owen."

And for her. It didn't take a genius to guess how much her family—all her family—adored her. You would have to be a fool not to. He set down his cup. "So, what went wrong with the marriage?"

"Hey, isn't that a little personal?"

"Sure, but we've got time. I'll tell you my troubles if you tell me yours."

"Like I would want to hear about your troubles." A glimmer of curiosity sparkled in her eyes. "What kind of problems can a carefree bachelor have?"

"You would be surprised." He went for humor because she looked as if she needed it to get her mind off her son. Time would fly faster that way and the surgeon would be walking in with good news before she knew it. "Women keep dumping me."

"Because you won't get serious with them."

"Sure, but I still get dumped. It's hard on a man's ego."

"You don't look like your ego is hurting any."

"You might be surprised. I spend a lot of Friday nights alone with my horse. It's sad."

"As opposed to scrubbing the kitchen floor after Owen goes to bed because it's the only uninterrupted time I have to clean?"

"See? I don't have anyone to scrub my kitchen floor. Poor me."

There. Now laughter was dancing in those beautiful gray eyes and hooking the corners of her mouth upward. She had to know he wasn't serious, because she didn't hike her bag off the floor and threaten to smack him with it, the way his sisters might have.

"Yes, poor you. I'm truly surprised you can't keep a girlfriend for long."

"I know. I can't figure it out. I'm heartbroken and lonely."

"Lonely? I don't believe it. C'mon, women must flock around you, I'm sure. They dump you eventually, but they are interested in you in the first place."

"There aren't as many as you think." He may as well tell the truth. "I spend the weekend with my horse, and a lot of ladies find fault with me for that."

"Jack is your best friend."

"That he is. A man can always count on his horse."

"I remember those days. My parents still

have my Patches, but I haven't had time to ride since I graduated from high school. That was a few years ago." Some of the strain eased from her face. The tension lines across her forehead vanished as she remembered. "I got Patches when I was twelve. He was one of the best friends I've ever had. I shared cookies and ice cream and secrets with him. He passed away a few years before Owen was born, and I miss him."

"I lost my first horse a while back. One of the saddest days of my life. Dagwood was the horse dad put me on when I was little. That horse and I bonded like glue. I have Jack now, but I still miss my first love." He twisted in the chair to face her. The wide warmth of his palm covered her hand. The contact was a zing of electric spark and a comforting sweetness that made her feel less alone. Should she take her hand away and break the contact? Or pretend as if he wasn't affecting her?

"What happened with Ricky?" His question was blunt but kind with concern. "I still don't get why he isn't here. I can't imagine anyone not caring about your boy. Even I do, and I hardly know him."

"Ricky." There was a difficult subject. Her chest seized up like a full-scale panic attack. The truth was hard, but there was no getting around it. "Ricky said he didn't want to be tied down anymore, so he left."

"He just decided to walk away?" Confusion twisted across Tucker's forehead and darkened his eyes.

"Life with me and Owen was tedious and nothing but work. So, Ricky left." That was all she wanted to say. Anything more, and it would be too overwhelming. She could just imagine that Tucker Granger, with his wandering lifestyle, would start sympathizing with her ex. "Good thing he got out when he did. Look at how serious and demanding our life has gotten."

Not a good attempt at lightness, but she wished it had been. She shrugged her shoulders, hoping to hide the deep sense of inadequacy she could not escape.

"Ricky's loss." He looked as if he meant it. Tucker had that strong, kind, honorable thing going on, an aura of integrity and grit that made her heart flutter a tiny bit. She had to be imagining things because Tucker Granger wasn't that kind of man.

Or was he? She couldn't think of a single reason why a carefree, nomadic bachelor would fight his way through a city slowed down by drifted snow to bring coffee and comfort to someone he hardly knew anymore—except for one. He was more caring than he seemed and more dependable than he wanted to admit.

Not in the same league with Ricky, not at all.

"I might not be a settling-down kind of a man," he said, grabbing his cup and lifting it as if in a toast. "But I know what matters in life. I'll sit right here with you as long as you need me to."

"Thanks, Tucker." Her throat tightened with gratitude that felt too big to hold back. She was strong. She could wait here on her own just fine, but having a friend at her side was nice and an old friend even better.

She remembered the boy he used to be, joking around in class and always ready with a wise-mouthed answer sure to make everyone laugh. But he had a serious side, too, a solid personality that maturity had given him, and she was grateful for that.

"Sierra?" A woman's voice cut through her thoughts and rose above the other muted conversations in the waiting area.

"Mom?" She twisted in her chair, elation spiraling through her at the sight of her mother, looking worse for the wear. Still wearing her winter parka and carting her carry-on luggage, the woman charged across the room. She hadn't even stopped at the hotel room.

"Baby, I stayed all night at the airport, I pleaded my case with the ticket agent and I got on the first flight out." Jeri Lynn set her suitcase against the wall and peeled off her gloves. "I'm here. How's our Owen?"

"So far, so good. At least they haven't told

me any differently." She felt Tucker's hand withdraw from hers and she couldn't explain why she felt bereft, why she felt unbearably lonely or why her hand continued to tingle with the memory of his comforting touch. Her mother was in her arms before she could ponder it too much.

"I can see I'm no longer needed." Kindness, strong and good, radiated from him as he clutched his cane and pushed himself to his feet. Was it her imagination or did he seem sad, too? In a blink the look in his eyes had changed and he was the same unstoppable, untamable force he'd always been. "Give me a call when Owen's in recovery. I want to hear how great his surgery went."

"I will." She caught that look in her mother's eye. The smart thing to do would be to wave the man away as if he meant nothing at all, as if they hadn't shared a moment of closeness, but that wouldn't be right. He was already striding away on those long, powerful legs of his, injury and all.

She managed to disentangle herself from her mother and step after him. "I can't tell you what it meant that you came. I—"

"Don't sweat it. I know." He winked like a man without a care in the world, but this time she wasn't fooled. She could see the layers beneath his dazzling, easygoing grin. He was worried about Owen, he was sad to be leaving and she didn't know how to ask him to stay. Maybe he didn't know how to ask either.

"Call me." Those were his last words to her before he turned away with a plea on his handsome face she would not soon forget.

He cared about Owen. And that made her like him far too much.

"Well, now, isn't this interesting?" Her mother sounded pleased with the situation. "That Granger boy came all this way to sit with you this morning. Maybe I should have taken a detour to the hotel, maybe showered, changed and searched down some coffee. That would have given you more time together."

"He was only being nice, Mother." Really. She hadn't been able to hold Ricky's attention. What chance did she have of keeping a man as handsome, vital and popular as Tucker? He lived a life full of constant change and excitement, even if he did confess to spending most of his nonwork time with his horse. She held no illusions. She was an average girl, and once she'd dreamed that a man could love her enough to change his ways. She would never make that mistake again.

"Tucker was Owen's charity wish, you know that. He came here this morning for Owen." She gave her mom one more hug before recovering her knitting, which she'd forgotten about. It had tumbled to the seat and a few stitches had slipped off. She bowed her head to fish the stitches back onto the needle. "Tucker brought extra coffee. Go ahead and help yourself to the latte."

"I will, bless him!" Mom settled into a chair with a smile on her face, but it could not surpass the worry in her eyes. They both knew they had a long wait ahead.

Sierra couldn't explain why she felt something was missing—why *someone* was missing. She resisted the urge to glance over her shoulder, knowing full well that Tucker was long gone, and that was the way it should be.

"How are you doing, son?"

Tucker adjusted the phone on his shoulder and considered his dad's question as he dropped the last of his clothes into his suitcase. His hotel windows offered a snowy, winter-wonderland view of downtown Denver, but the scenery wasn't what he saw. It was Sierra sitting alone in the waiting room with her knitting in her lap and anguish on her beautiful face. He hadn't liked walking away, but he didn't belong there. Her family had that right. If he'd stayed it would have only gotten complicated.

"I'm packing right now. Catching a plane in a few hours." He added his shaving kit to the mess, closed the lid and strong-armed the zipper closed.

"Great news. I'll pick you up at the airport. Get more time with my son that way." Dad sounded warm as always but there was something else layered in his words. Something that tugged at Tucker, bringing up all kinds of issues he didn't want to face. He found life was easier staying on the surface. Or it had been until the accident. He'd been bucked off a bareback bronc the same way he had hundreds of times, but this landing had been different. He'd flown directly into the horse's path and the animal hadn't been able to avoid him.

Pain. That was the first thing he remembered before his heart had stopped beating. He'd been officially dead for two minutes and thirty-odd seconds until paramedics had gotten his ticker going again. Those two minutes had changed everything.

Including him.

"I'd like that, Dad." When he had woken up in ICU, his father had been at his side.

He knew he'd put his dad through a lot of fear and worry, and he was sorry for it. He'd been able to spend ample time at home on the family ranch recuperating, and he'd gotten used to seeing his father every day. He missed him now. "I'll text you my flight information."

"Great. Any word on how the little Baker boy is doing?" Caring about others, that was Frank Granger. Sincerity rang deep in his baritone as his light tone fell away, leaving only solemness. "He was first on my morning's list of prayers."

"Mine, too." He swallowed hard, ignoring the tug of worry deep in his gut. The image of the little kid, with one arm around Slayer and his eyes wide with excitement listening to rodeo stories, stuck with him. *Lord, please watch over that boy.*

"I haven't heard anything. You know what they say. No news is good news." The tug of worry worsened. He couldn't help being worried. It was impossible not to care about

Owen. "Sierra promised to call me when there's news."

"Then you can update me." Whatever Frank said next was interrupted by an electronic beep.

A check of the screen told him he had an incoming call. "Dad, I have to go. Sierra's on the line."

"See you soon, son."

He clicked the phone over, unable to explain why his heart began to hammer and his palms went damp. "Sierra?"

"He's fine. He's in recovery." Her words came in a rush, driven by relief and thankfulness. "The surgeon said it couldn't have gone better."

"See? What did I tell you." The smile splitting his face was nothing compared to the joy uplifting him. He grabbed the suitcase by the handle and lowered it to the floor. "I'm sure he will be out of that hospital and back home in no time."

"That's the plan. I can't see him yet, but it won't be much longer." Her warmth somehow flowed through the phone line, the tangible gentleness that he'd experienced in her presence. "Thank you for all you did for him. You made my son one happy little boy. That made a difference going into this surgery."

"I didn't know that I did all that much. Nothing at all, when compared to what you do for him." The need to see her gripped him hard. He wanted to be sure she was all right. He knew her mother was there to take care of her, but the need remained. He could picture the relief on her beautiful face, the love lighting her eyes, the joy polishing her. He swallowed hard, doing his best to push aside that pretty picture. "I hope you take good care of yourself, too. No long nights without sleep. No skipping meals."

"That's what I have my mom for. She's been watching over me." Sierra laughed, as if her mother was close, and sure enough there came a woman's muffled response. Sierra laughed again. "My mom wanted you to know she's well equipped for that job.

Chip and Betty made it in a little bit ago, and you know my mother-in-law. She keeps trying to feed me."

"Then I can leave town in good conscience knowing you are in good hands." His throat tried to close up at the thought of leaving. Funny, because that didn't make a lick of sense. He never had problems leaving a female behind. Staying always put him in a panicked sweat.

"Have a safe flight home." Her voice dipped low as if she were trying to keep her mother from overhearing. "Thanks for coming to sit with me this morning. I can't tell you what that meant."

"For me, too." That was only the truth. He was glad he'd helped out. Life was a finite gift and how a man spent his time mattered. He grabbed his cane from the bedside table. "Have Owen give me a call when he's up to it. I'll need to keep him updated on my sheep search."

"Then I guess I will be seeing you again, Tucker Granger."

He couldn't help liking the note of respect he heard, respect he had in turn for her. "I guess this isn't over. Are you sure you want your son to grow up to be a rodeo cowboy?"

"I want my son to grow up well and happy, and I'll be thankful with that." A world of love vibrated in her words. "Goodbye, Tucker."

"Adios." He kept his tone light but what he felt wasn't light at all. Not in the least. He tucked his phone into his pocket, leaned his weight on the cane and grabbed the suitcase handle. He limped to the door, wheeling his luggage after him. He shut out the lights and took one last look around. Yep, he got everything—nothing was left behind. He stepped into the hallway, unable to sidestep the feeling that he was missing something. The feeling followed him all the way home.

Chapter Five

"Look who is home." His older sister, Autumn, rode up to the garage on her chestnut-bay mare, her strawberry-blond ponytail bouncing behind her in the brisk, wintry wind. "I hear little Owen is doing just fine. Already talking about coming home."

Tucker hopped down from the passenger side of the truck and grabbed his cane. News traveled fast in a small town and he was fairly sure which way the wind was blowing. Good thing his two younger sisters, Cheyenne and Addison, were away at school or he would never hear the end of it. To make matters worse, Dad was behind the wheel paying close attention.

Great. Nothing like everyone thinking they knew your business. He tugged the suitcase from the backseat, fairly sure he could figure out what they were all thinking. With his older brother's recent wedding and Autumn's engagement, the family was probably hearing wedding bells for him and Sierra.

Play it down, he thought. Best to act as if this is all no big deal. The suitcase hit concrete with a thud and he closed the truck door. "I heard the same thing. Glad the little fella is going to be okay."

"I also found out something *very* interesting." Autumn stripped off her gloves, and the diamond ring she wore glinted in the late afternoon sunlight.

"Great. Whatever it is, I don't need to hear it." He tossed a dimpled grin at his sister, hoping to distract her. "You know I'm not the romantic sort. I don't want to hear about your love life, Autumn. Sorry. I'm not your confidant."

She looked confused, her forehead crinkling, her mouth twisting down in the corners. She planted both hands on the saddle horn and stared him up and down like he was a bull in a china shop. He figured he had about two more seconds before she figured out he'd said something that made no sense on purpose to derail her, so he had better start moving as fast as his injured leg would allow. He wanted to be in the house before she brought up the issue of Sierra Baker again.

"Why are you movin' so fast, son?" Dad was a sharp tack, and silent laughter lit up his face as he ambled behind Tucker along the pathway to the back porch. "I haven't seen you get a move on like that since you were sixteen and stole Autumn's truck keys."

"I borrowed them." Another infamous story about him that hadn't died down, even more than a decade later. "There were extenuating circumstances."

"There always are." Frank's chuckle was a sound that had defined Tucker's childhood and the rumble of it now made him smile. He couldn't help it. He had a lifetime of laughing with his dad, of sharing the same honest good humor. But he currently didn't have time to let the memories surge up because of the sharp, rapid knell of steeled horse hoofs beating behind him and gaining ground.

Uh-oh. He glanced over his shoulder to see his sister with a determined look on her face and an unyielding jut of her chin. His tactic hadn't worked as long as he'd hoped. May as well brace for the worst.

"I heard from my friend Caroline directly from Terri that her mother heard all about how Sierra's mom found you two cozied up together in the hospital waiting room."

Cozied up? It was worse than he'd suspected. His chest squeezed tight in the first stages of panic. Was it too late to do damage control? He glanced out of the corner of his eye at his dad. It was hard to miss the burst of pleasure lighting Frank up like a Fourth of July fireworks display.

"Is that true, Tucker?" His father clomped up the steps behind him. "Is there something you want to tell us about you and Sierra?"

Definitely too late. Grimacing, he launched across the porch and yanked open the door. "My flight out was delayed, so I went by the hospital to check on the kid. That's the extent of it."

"You thought you were safe from prying eyes in Denver. Wrong." Autumn's big-sister amusement didn't end. "I think you should go for it. Sierra is about the nicest person I know. She would make you a good wife."

"I brought her a cup of coffee, not a diamond ring." He sat down to kick off his boots on the bench by the back door and heard the telltale creak of leather as she dismounted. His sister intended to follow him into the house. Sure enough, her step tapped across the porch. Why couldn't she just stay on her horse and let this lie?

Dad sat down beside him and heaved off his right boot. "Looks like you're in trouble, son. Now everybody is going to think you're sweet on the girl."

"On Sierra?" He grimaced again, mostly because his heart beat oddly at the sound of her name. "You know me. I'm sweet on all the girls."

"Disgusting." The corners of Autumn's mouth fought a grin as she charged into the mudroom. "I can't believe we're related."

"I'm just not the settling-down type." A standard line, so he used it, knowing his sister would sail on by with a shake of her head, which she did, and his dad would blow out a frustrated sigh, which he did.

"One day some pretty gal will lasso you by the heart and you won't have any more excuses." Dad hauled off his left boot and stood. "I've got a few calls to make, and then I'm heading to town. Need to stop by the feed store. Want to come?"

"Sure." His chest ached with both memories and longings he didn't want to name. It was good to be home, good to accompany his dad on errands, just like he used to do when he was a boy.

His cell chose that moment to ring, merrily jingling an electronic tune. He pulled it out of his pocket and winced when he saw the screen.

"Is it her?" Autumn reappeared with a travel mug in hand, probably full of hot tea. "Be careful. I think I hear wedding bells."

"Funny." He shook his head and waited until his sister was safely out the door before he took the call. "Hi, Sierra."

"Nope, it's me."

At the sound of that weak little voice, Tucker hopped off the bench, relief hitting him like a speeding train. "Owen. It's good to hear from you, buddy."

"Did you hear that, Mom? Tucker and me are buddies." Sierra's pleasant alto rang in the distance and Owen came on the line again. "I'm all better now. They fixed up the hole."

"Excellent job. I hear you wowed that surgeon. You must have been the best patient he's ever had."

"Yep. I got Slayer and Jack with me. I'm gonna be home real soon."

"That's great." Tucker strolled into the kitchen, cane in hand, and caught his father trying to listen. Frank didn't turn his head away fast enough and nearly dropped the cordless handset. He hoped his dad hadn't caught a glimpse of the truth—a truth Tucker wasn't entirely comfortable with. The kid affected him deep in the heart, and Sierra—

He'd best stop thinking of her.

"Say good-bye, Owen." Her voice, although background, became the focus.

His senses sharpened and he found himself stalled dead center in the kitchen because his brain had lost the concentration necessary to keep walking. When she spoke again, a hook latched into him and reeled in his attention against every bit of his will.

"You need your rest, baby." Love polished her words until they shone with brightness even he could see. "Tucker understands that. Now, tell him good-bye and hang up. You can call him later, I'm sure."

"Okay." The boy drew out the single word in a long sigh. "Tucker, gotta go. Talk to my mom."

Sierra? The panic Tucker fought amped up a notch. Being with her at the hospital had felt right—too right. He wasn't comfortable with that. His palms went damp as he heard her gasp in surprise.

"No, I don't—" She didn't complete the sentence.

That was okay, because he could do it for her. She didn't want to talk to him. She would rather avoid him. And that got him thinking she must have really been desperate this morning to have been glad for his company in those early hours of Owen's surgery. He couldn't say exactly why hurt shot through him. He didn't want to care about the woman. He didn't want to like her.

The plain fact was he did.

"Mom." Owen sounded unhappy and

it didn't take much to imagine the boy stretched out in his hospital bed, hooked up to IVs and weak from his ordeal, holding out the phone for his mother to take against her wishes.

He tried not to imagine Sierra's grimace as she took the phone or the reluctance she might be feeling at being forced to talk to him again. He remembered the first look she'd thrown him when he'd walked into the hospital straight from the airport and had seen her waiting for him, pale with worry and exhaustion. She couldn't hide the gentle scorn she held generally for a man like him. He feared it had returned and she wouldn't be able to disguise it now.

"Tucker." She had a beautiful alto, the kind of voice made for singing in church choirs and for lulling babies to sleep. The kind of voice that could make even a man like him dream just a tad. She didn't sound disdainful, but she didn't sound comfortable either. "I hope we haven't bothered you.

Owen insisted, and right now I can't say no to him."

"I understand. Glad to hear from him. I mean that." His voice dipped, knowing full well that though his dad had retreated to the living room he was still in eavesdropping range. "Owen is a good kid. He can call me anytime."

"I'll let him know." She sounded shaky, as if she were on the verge of tears.

She had to be exhausted, up with worry most of last night and still going strong taking care of her boy. A powerful urge to look after her returned stronger than ever, and he couldn't explain it.

"Take care, Tucker. Thank you again."

"My pleasure." And it had been. He listened to the click as she disconnected before taking the phone from his ear.

Unfamiliar emotions left him unable to move. He listened to the rumble of Dad's baritone from the neighboring room and the tap of the housekeeper, Mrs. Gunderson, as she marched into sight with a loaded laundry basket braced on one hip. Still, he could not force one foot forward.

He didn't like the grip Sierra Baker had on him. No, he didn't like it at all.

"I can't believe you're back home so early." The reverend's wife, Doris, stood on Sierra's front step, bundled against the January wind, with a covered casserole in hand. "They don't keep anyone very long in a hospital these days."

"Come in out of the cold." Snowflakes danced in the air and chased her into the trailer as Sierra held the door open wide for her guest. The heaters clicked on and ruffled the window curtains in the living room. Their young dog, Puddles, barked from the couch, curled up with Owen. "I can't believe you braved the snow to visit us."

"I had to see how Owen was and to deliver this casserole." Doris ushered herself straight to the small galley kitchen and slid the dish onto the counter. "Owen, did you get taller in that hospital? You look bigger to me. Did you start lifting weights?"

"No, ma'am. I'm just me." Owen sat up on the couch, rubbed his eyes awake from the nap he was supposed to be taking and held his yellow Lab tight. "But I am gonna be a champion rodeo rider."

"Is that so?"

"Yep. My new friend Tucker's gonna teach me." Owen beamed and the Lab panted as if in encouragement.

"Tucker, huh?" It was hard to miss that sly, knowing look on Doris's face. She un-buttoned her winter coat. "I hear he paid a visit to your hospital room. He was a real comfort to you and your mama."

"Yes, ma'am." Owen nodded earnestly, his dark locks dropping across his forehead and into his big blue eyes. He was still recover-ing from his operation, but the surgery had corrected so many things—his coloring, his difficulty breathing and his energy level.

She was deeply grateful to the Lord for that.

"Tucker Granger was a comfort to *Owen*." Sierra emphasized as she took Doris's coat. "*Not* to me."

"Sure. Why would a handsome young man be a comfort to you?" Doris let her eyes twinkle merrily.

"Owen, lie back. You need to rest." Sierra concentrated on what mattered—her son. It wasn't easy tucking away thoughts of Tucker Granger. She couldn't explain the impact he'd had on her. Maybe it was best not to analyze it too much.

"But, Mom, you said we could play a rodeo tape." Owen sounded brittle, although he was fighting so hard to pretend he wasn't tired. He had a lot of healing to do, poor boy. The dog licked his face.

"I'll find a tape." She gave thanks again that her mother had recorded several of Owen's favorite shows off her satellite, anticipating the bed rest to come. "You lie back, now."

"Tucker said even he had to rest up to heal." Owen didn't move, stretching to see which cassette she was pulling off the small shelf beneath the handed-down TV. Puddles scented the air. Something smelled good. "Mom, can I see the one where Tucker is riding Jack? Please?"

"I think this is it." She felt Doris's amusement as she slid the tape into the VCR and hit the button. The antenna reception blinked off and the sights and sounds of a rodeo filled the small room. Oh, it was good to have her child home safe and sound. God was very good indeed. She handed her little boy the remote and helped him to lie back on the couch.

"There he is!" Fascinated, Owen didn't blink as his hero on horseback rode onto the screen.

"Isn't that cute?" Doris whispered. "Any word from Ricky?"

Sierra shook her head. Not even a call to see if his son had made it through all right. Didn't that say enough about the man's priorities?

One thing was sure, she could never make

a mistake like that again. Her heart wasn't the only one at stake. She watched her little boy wrap his arm around his stuffed bull and hold on tight, lost in the excitement. Applause roared from the TV speakers and an announcer commented on Tucker's aptitude as an all-around cowboy.

Her heart ached in the strangest way remembering what he had done for her son.

"Is that a car door I hear? Goodness, I wasn't the only one who noticed you were home." Doris sounded surprised as she opened the door. Delicate snowflakes rode in on a bitter wind. The puppy barked again. "Look who it is. Cady Winslow with two big bags of groceries. Cady, let me take one of those. They look heavy."

"They are." The tall, elegant middle-aged newcomer to town hurried in. Snow clung to her brown curls and long eyelashes. "It's really starting to come down out there. Hi, Sierra. I noticed your car was in the driveway on my way to town, so I picked up a few things for you."

"You shouldn't have." Her throat thickened until it was hard to talk. "You went to a lot of trouble."

"Not at all. I was shopping for myself anyway. It was easy to pick up another carton of milk and eggs." Cady set the bag on the counter next to the one Doris had left. "I figured you might not be able to make it to the store because of Owen. I took care of my mother for years, so I know how it can be. It's impossible to do everything at once. Let me get the cold things in the fridge for you."

As if everyone's prayers hadn't been enough, this brought tears to her eyes. She didn't know how she could ever pay back such kindness toward her son.

"Say, Cady." Doris had that sly look again. "How are the preparations going for your open house?"

"It's a lot to do, but it should all be done by Valentine's Day." Cady unwound her scarf, not looking the least bit harried. She had bought and renovated the local inn, which had been vacant for years, and her scheduled opening day was coming up quickly. "We're on schedule. So far, so good."

"You speak up and let me know if you need any help, even if it's last minute." Doris appeared happy at the prospect. "If there's one thing I love, it's a party. Tell me how your hiring is coming along."

Thank goodness Doris had another victim to extract information from. Sierra happily slipped into the galley kitchen to turn up the burner beneath the teakettle.

Another knock sounded at the door, the Lab barked and the knob turned. "Hello, there. I didn't know there would be a crowd here." Her sister-in-law Terri bustled in with a grocery sack in one hand and a covered casserole in the other. "I guess we all had the same idea. Brace yourself, Sierra, because my mom isn't far behind me."

"And mine probably isn't far behind her." She hurried to take the grocery sack from Terri, relieved to see her. "Oh, and you brought a container of cookies for Owen."

"I made his favorite this morning." Terri beamed. "Time to spoil my nephew. Oh, he looks good. We have the whole town praying for him."

"Those prayers made a difference." Sierra let the bag come to a rest on the counter, gazing love-struck at her little boy watching the screen with a look of utter life and joy on his dear, button face. The dog watched alongside him.

"How did his visit with his favorite rodeo star go?" Terri chuckled just a hint, as if she already knew the answer.

"Tucker Granger was very good and generous." She hoped she wasn't blushing. "Owen will hardly put down that stuffed bull Tucker gave him."

"I hear Mr. Gorgeous and Available was also very good to you."

"He was only being kind. That's it." She may as well admit the whole truth to herself. She'd glimpsed a part of the man that had intrigued and touched her, a part she admired. She liked him. "He was more thoughtful than I would have expected, but you all know Tucker. As soon as his leg heals up, he will be gone from this town like the wind."

"Nothing can tie a man down if he doesn't want to be." Terri nodded with understanding. "Maybe one day the right man will come along for you."

"I'm not looking for a man." She watched Owen grin up at Cady as she sat on the opposite cushion and leaned in to pet Puddles. Owen began explaining all about the rodeo.

Her son was her one true love, the center of her life. She never wanted to put her faith in another man, no matter how solid. She couldn't do that to herself and especially to Owen. She would never forget how her little boy had cried in the middle of the night for his father for nearly an entire year. And, most recently, there was Owen's quiet disappointment when Ricky had decided not to show up at the hospital.

Her son had been let down enough. She

had to protect him from another man who might disappoint him. Across the room, Cady asked a question and Owen pointed to the screen to answer it.

"I have everything I need to be happy." A week ago, she had been terrified she would lose him. God had seen them safely through and she would not forget the lesson she had been reminded of. Owen mattered, nothing else. Whatever was missing in her life wasn't as important as what she already had.

"I'll come over tomorrow and stay with Owen. I'll bring Toby." Terri smiled at the mention of her dog. "I know you start early at the diner."

"Thanks for watching him." She had to go back to work. Her meager savings had gone as far as it could go, her bank account was nearly empty and her credit cards maxed. "As soon as the doctor clears him, he can go back to the church's day care."

"No hurry. I like to spend time with my nephew." Terri whisked her casserole to the refrigerator and slipped it onto an empty shelf. "I hear a car in the driveway. Looks like Mom is here. You're going to have a full house before long."

"Bring it on." Sierra felt lighter than she had in months. So much was going right in her life. She had many blessings and she was grateful for every one.

As for Tucker, what she felt for him was friendship. That's all it would ever be. The water was boiling, so she plucked the kettle off the stove and began filling cups. The fragrance of steeping tea steamed upward. The door opened and both her mom and mother-in-law piled in, exclaiming about the weather and the Granger men they'd talked to on Main Street before heading over.

Tucker. Thoughts of him warmed her like sweet tea. The impact of his kindness remained like a tie she could not break.

Chapter Six

"Look who just walked in. Be still my heart." Sandi Walters abandoned the grill, where hamburgers for the lunchtime crowd were sizzling. She laid a hand to her throat. The middle-aged woman gaped in adoration at the oldest of the trio of men who ambled through the diner's front door.

Sierra had a heart-stalling moment of her own. Tucker looked better than she'd remembered with his dark brown hair wind tousled, snow flocking the broad shoulders of his black parka. He had a manly presence a woman could drown in, even a woman who didn't want a man, much less a wandering one. Was she in big trouble?

Definitely. But she would like anyone who had been so good to her son. Maybe that's all this feeling was, a deep gratitude and appreciation for Tucker's altruism. Nothing to worry about whatsoever.

"That Frank Granger." Sandi roused herself out of her daze, grabbed her spatula and turned her attention to the grill. "He takes my breath away whenever he's near and at my age that's an unsettling thing. I about go into some sort of health crisis every time."

"Maybe it's something in the Granger men's DNA that makes them so dazzling." Since it wasn't busy, she couldn't delay facing one particular Granger man. She whipped her notepad out of her apron pocket, steeled her spine and tapped down the aisle. Was it her imagination or had every eye in the place turned to watch her progress toward the booth where the Grangers settled in?

Probably her imagination. She lifted her chin, skidded to a stop on her rubber-soled shoes and did her best not to look at Tucker at all. She focused on his dad instead, just as she always did. "Hi, Frank. Your usual, or do you want to hear the specials?"

"I've got a hankering for my usual cheeseburger. Do you boys know what you want?"

Out of the corner of her eye, she saw the oldest brother flip open the table menu, glance over the offerings and order the same. The wedding ring on his hand caught the overhead light. Justin looked relaxed and happy. Marriage suited him well. He was the stable older brother, a man just like his father. The staying kind.

Unlike the younger brother, who cleared his throat, tossed the menu at Justin to put away behind the napkin canister and planted his elbows on the edge of the table. "Let's hear the specials."

Was it her imagination or had the diner gone completely silent as if everyone watched breathlessly? She scribbled on her pad, avoided looking directly at Tucker and dreaded what would happen if their gazes met. She could feel the dozen pairs of eyes taking in every movement, every look on her face. There wasn't enough entertainment in this town. Folks should get iPods or talk on their cell phones or something. She felt painfully on display.

"We have a roast beef sandwich with steak fries and coleslaw." She felt awkward and stared at her notepad. She was uncomfortable with her feelings about the man and feared it might show. "There's also a chicken and dumplings plate that is very good. It's Sandi's specialty."

"Bring that, please. I have a fondness for dumplings." The quality of the smile in his voice lured her with a promise of friendship.

Her gaze lifted from the notepad against her wishes, pulled by some indefinable quality in the man she could not refuse. The snow gently falling in the window behind him hazed into a background whiteness and vanished, the same way the rest of the diner did and the people in it. There was only the two of them. Against her will, she recalled the comfort his touch had given her.

"Chicken and dumplings it is." Her voice croaked, and although she cleared her throat it made no difference. "What would you like to drink?"

"Bring us three colas, gal," Frank answered, sounding amused but in a kindly way, as if he saw everything far too clearly.

Heat blazed across her face, and she scribbled down the rest of the order. The diner remained silent, except for a faint clank from the kitchen as Sandi plated orders. Sierra clicked her pen and tucked it into her front pocket. "Anything else?"

"How is Owen doing?" Tucker's impossibly blue eyes speared hers, holding her captive and showing his genuine concern.

Her uneasiness melted. The distance she wanted between them vanished. "He's good. He isn't happy to be banished to the couch, but he feels well enough to complain about it. Thankfully."

"Excellent." Dimples bracketed his smile, making him irresistible. There was definitely something powerful in the Granger men's DNA. He leaned closer, conspiratorially. "Is it my imagination, or is this place unusually quiet?"

"No, it's quiet."

"I suppose everyone's concerned about Owen's recuperation. But I think that isn't all folks are wondering about." He leaned back against the booth cushion and glanced around. A lot of guilty faces turned away with knowing smirks. He laughed. "I can hear the speculation from here. Is it me, or have you heard the rumors, too?"

"I've heard those rumors." Her gray eyes brightened with humor and soul. "I suspect everyone is watching to see just how true they are."

"As if folks don't know me by now. I'm not a settling-down type, so why does everyone have us practically dating?" He shot a glance at his dad, hoping the man would get a clue.

"I have no idea." When Sierra smiled full-on without reserve, it was a sight to behold. "As if folks think I would settle for the likes of you."

Never had he seen a more beautiful woman. Never had he witnessed grace and sweetness wrapped up together before. He didn't like the way his spirit turned toward her or the fact that his father was right. He more than liked the woman. He didn't like that fact either.

"Only a dimwit would think a fine lady like you would hold the slightest fondness for a lout like me." He threw his voice just enough so that everyone in the diner could hear. "I'm trouble. You are wise enough to know that."

"I certainly am." She rolled her eyes, shook her head and ripped the top sheet off her notepad. "You are far below my standards, Tucker."

"I know I am. I can't understand why everyone can't see it." He liked the way she conspired with him. He didn't like the syrupy, strangely happy emotion seeping into him as he shared a chuckle with her. "I don't see how you can lower yourself to talk to me at all."

"Believe me, it's a struggle." She turned on her heels and the gray loveliness of the daylight followed her the same way his spirit did, unable to let go as she padded up the aisle. Clearly, she did not have similar feelings for him.

What a relief. So why did the memory of her laughter and the happiness it brought him remain after she was out of his sight?

"You and Tucker really aren't an item?" Sandi asked in a low whisper as she built Frank's cheeseburger. "I'm disappointed. I was rootin' for you, girl."

"Why is this such a big deal?" She tore off her latest order and entered it into the computer. "I don't understand."

"You are beloved around here, don't you know that by now?" Sandi dropped the top bun on the burger and gave the plate a shove. "Everyone saw how bad you were hurt when Ricky up and left you. I've had a marriage go bad, so I know that pain. I'm sure this whole town, like me, has been praying for something good to come into your life. You've had a hard row, honey, that's all. I say it's about time for things to turn around."

"Thank you, Sandi." Her throat felt tight as she grabbed Frank's plate. She'd had some hard times over the past few years, but she'd never been alone in this friendly, small town, not once. It strengthened her as she grabbed the two waiting plates and circled through the open doorway.

Her thoughts boomeranged to her son, who had stayed on her mind all morning long. She hated being away from him. She knew he was in capable hands, but that didn't make the ill feeling in her stomach go away.

"Need some more ketchup, dear," Mrs. Tipple called out. "I know you're busy."

Sierra paused in her tracks to smile at

the sweet, elderly widow, seated with her friends from church. "I'll get right on it. Do you ladies need me to refill your iced teas?"

"Oh, no, we're fine," they all chorused, merry as larks, and Sierra went on her way toward the Granger booth. The three men talked away, Tucker chuckling at something his dad said.

"Sierra!" Frank reached out to take his plate from her. "Just in time. I was about to eat my boot. The boys and I have been talking."

"Uh-oh. That sounds like trouble to me." She slid Justin's plate onto the table and told herself there was no need to dread facing Tucker. The man grinned up at her the way he always did, easygoing, as if he didn't have a care in the world. Except now she knew him enough to read the shadows in his lapis-blue eyes.

He was only being nice to you at the hospital. She had to remember that. She eased his plate in front of him, ignoring the hitch in her chest and his leather-and-winter scent.

"We got the sheep all lined up for your boy." Frank stole a steak fry from his plate. "Although Tucker says it might be a while before Owen gets the go-ahead from the doc to ride, we're making all the preparations. I hear he's been pretty excited about the prospect."

"Excited? It's all he talks about. Tucker, you gave him something positive to focus on. It's helped him."

"Good. My family has had a lot of reminders lately how blessed we are." Tucker's words rumbled with honesty, a very attractive quality. It was hard to remember she'd ever had a low opinion of him. As he reached for his cola, he said, "We've been talking, and my dad suggested Owen might want to go for a ride on Jack before he wrangles a few sheep."

"Your dad suggested it." It sounded like something Frank would think of. Frank, not Tucker. She had to remember that. She drew in a slow breath to steady herself, so the sting of disappointment wouldn't show. Disappointment made no sense, but she felt it anyway. "Owen would love it. You know how he gets so excited about your rodeo horse."

"He can learn a few things about riding before he tries mutton busting. That was Autumn's idea."

"Mutton busting?"

"Riding sheep." Tucker took a sip, watching her over the rim of the glass.

This wasn't a personal invitation. This came from all of the Grangers and it made it easier to accept. She took a step back, remembering her other duties. "Owen will love it."

"Then it's settled." It was Frank's turn to speak up. "Give us a call when the doc gives the go-ahead. We'll be looking forward to it."

"We will, too." Another step took her farther away from the table and away from

Tucker. She grabbed a fresh ketchup bottle for Mrs. Tipple.

Could she help it if her gaze went back to him? He bowed his head as his father led the prayer. She had a good view of him over the back of the booth as she set the bottle on the elderly ladies' table. The sincere low murmur of his amen rumbled like winter thunder. It was gratitude she felt for the man, nothing more.

"Thank you, dear." Mrs. Tipple smiled up at her, a lifetime of beauty on her face. "I heard from Cady Winslow that the doctor who diagnosed your son is coming out for another visit. Isn't that nice?"

"Oh, it certainly is." Just what she needed to refocus. "Doctor Stone must be coming for the inn's opening."

"I hear he and his girls made the very first booking. He is such a nice man." Mrs. Tipple beamed. "And so smart, since he helped your little Owen."

"He's unmarried," Mrs. Plum chimed in. "I hear his wife left him for his best friend.

What a shame. It had to have broken his heart."

"I'm sure it did." Uh-oh. Maybe this change of conversation wasn't an improvement. "Don't tell me you three ladies are still trying to marry me off?"

"Okay, we won't tell you." Mrs. Tipple chuckled.

"Although we are," Mrs. Parnell spoke up. "You work hard taking care of your little boy on your own. We want you to be happy, honey."

"Then please let me stay single." The joke made the three ladies laugh with amusement, but out of the corner of her eye she saw Tucker turn away as if he'd been watching her. Whether it was relief on his face at her comment or something else, she couldn't say.

It was dark when she pulled into her driveway. The headlights of her second-hand SUV swept through the pitch-black of the snowy evening. The windshield wipers swiped at the dizzying rush of snow, making it hard to see the gravel driveway. Exhaustion hung on her like an overlarge coat as she pulled into the carport and turned off the engine.

Silence surrounded her and she was too numb to think as she grabbed her purse, opened the door and met the bracing wind. It had been a long day. Her feet ached as she tripped up the steps to the front door. Her back complained, but she ignored it as she stepped into the welcoming warmth.

"Mom!" Owen sat up on the couch and swung his stockinged feet onto the floor. He pushed onto his feet, Slayer tucked into the crook of his arm. "Gramma said I could call Tucker today, and you know what? It's cuz we're buddies."

"So I've heard." Sierra tossed a smile at her mom, who sat in the recliner facing the TV, and dropped her keys and purse on the corner of the dinette. "I hope you aren't bothering Tucker."

"Nope. I gotta report in." Owen ambled

across the room, his free arm flying out. "Tucker said."

She knelt in time to wrap him into a sweet hug. Infinite love welled up within her. Life was simple when she walked through that door. Owen was her purpose in life and every last piece of her heart. She wanted to hold on to him forever. She breathed in the sweet, sugary scent of little boy and faint traces of cocoa. It wasn't easy to unwrap her arms from around his back and to feel his hand slip away from her neck. She wanted to protect him from every harm and hurt, no matter what it cost her. She ruffled his brown hair with her fingertips. "What do you report on?"

"That I ate all my vegetables, even the yucky broccoli." Squeezing Slayer, he backed away, his feet plodding on the carpet. "Right, Gramma?"

"Right." Jeri Lynn looked up from her knitting project with a smile. "I was amazed at how that boy tackled his greens. He was like a superhero."

"I was." Owen beamed. "Tucker always eats his broccoli. It's his supersecret. That's how he wins at the rodeo."

"That's pretty awesome he shared his secret with you." Another reason why she had to like the man, although that was no longer a hardship. "Do you want to know another secret to winning a rodeo?"

"Sure!"

"Getting a good night's sleep."

"Aw, Mom." Owen rolled his eyes with good-natured exaggeration.

Cute. "Go brush your teeth."

She waited until he ambled out of sight, resisting the urge to follow him every step of the way and hover over him. Owen might be healing just fine from his surgery, but she was having a harder time healing her fear of losing him.

"It will get easier." Jeri Lynn tucked away her knitting and rose from the comfortable chair. "I didn't let you out of my sight for nearly three months after you fell off your pony and cracked your head wide open. Do you remember?"

"How could I forget having to stay home while all my friends went riding." She eased out of her coat and hung it in the little entry closet. "Don't tell me that was more for your benefit than mine?"

"Half-and-half." She sidled close to slip her coat off a hanger. "You look beat. Hard day?"

"Long day. Mom, did you clean?"

"And did all the laundry, too. Terri did the hard work caring for Owen all day. By the time I got here, everything had been done, so I had to make myself useful." Jeri Lynn leaned close to brush a kiss against Sierra's cheek. "Don't you do a speck of housework. That's an order. You put your son to bed and that's it. Tomorrow I want to hear how you collapsed in front of the TV and took some downtime."

"I'll see what I can do." Not only did she have the best son but the best mom. She opened the door. "Drive safe."

"I certainly will. What a winter we're having! It started early and it's still going." Jeri Lynn zipped her parka in the spill of the porch light. "Good night, sweetheart."

"Thanks, Mom."

"Anytime."

Life was an interesting balance of good and hardship, of love and sorrow, and she was glad for this moment in time when her son was recovering, her mom was well and the rest of her family was fine. Snow dappled the window as she watched her mom make it to the four-wheel-drive. Headlights burst to life, Mom's blue mitten waved a final good-bye behind the dim windshield and the Jeep chugged into the storm until it disappeared completely.

"Mom! I'm done." Owen's call pulled her around and down the short hall into his little room. He padded around his bed in his red flannel pajamas and settled the Jack replica on his nightstand. "When I grow up, I'm gonna have a horse just like this."

"You are? What are you going to name

him?" She turned back the edge of his flannel sheets. "Wait, don't tell me—"

"Jack!" Owen burst out. It was good to see him full of hopes and she prayed he would always be just this way, open of heart and joyful of life. "I'm gonna ride him in the—"

"Rodeo," they said together, and she patted the mattress. "In you go."

"Mom?" Owen bounced onto the bed and tucked his feet beneath the covers she held for him. "Do you think I can be as good as Tucker one day?"

"I think you can be twice as good."

"Whew. Cuz then when I'm a big rodeo champion, Dad will want to see me win. He'll come then." Owen laid back on the pillow, Slayer tight in the crook of his arm. "He'll come."

"Oh, baby." Daggers to her heart could not hurt as much. She did not know how to protect him from what hurt most in life. She brushed silken, wayward strands from his forehead, fighting for composure. "Your daddy loves you. He's having a hard time showing it."

"One day I can fix it." Owen squeezed Slayer a little tighter. "I put it in my prayers."

At a loss, she watched her son steeple his hands and close his eyes. His rosebud mouth moved rapidly with silent prayers.

Hear him, Lord, she added one of her own. *Please heal his heart in all ways.*

The wind gusted against the side of the trailer and snow beat on the window. Owen opened his eyes, snuggled into his sheets and whispered good-night, ready to dream.

Chapter Seven

Cady Winslow knelt to gather towels off the concrete floor in one of the Grangers' horse stables when she felt a telltale bump against her forehead, the feather of whiskers and the brush of a velvety bottom lip. Her red cap popped off her head before she could try to save it. She glanced up, already laughing. Her palomino mare, Misty, lifted her head high, holding the knit hat between her front teeth like a prize.

"You funny girl." She abandoned the towels to pat the mare's neck affectionately, happiness making her feel half her age of fifty—not that she wanted to think on that too hard. She loved the satin warmth of the horse's light gold coat and the ripple of her pure white mane as Misty bobbed her head, intentionally keeping the cap out of reach. Big brown eyes beamed with delight.

"What do you have there? And however am I going to get it?" Her words made the mare happier, and the animal arched her neck proudly.

All her life Cady had wanted a horse. Moving from New York to Wyoming had been a big change, one she worried about at the time, but every day brought more reasons why the decision to leave the law firm behind had been an excellent one. Buying Misty and learning to ride her was the best happiness she'd experienced in a long time.

"I see she's playing her favorite game again." A rich, mature baritone vibrated good-natured amusement.

Cady didn't need to turn around to know who belonged to the smoky, resonate voice. It could only be Frank Granger because her heart had forgotten to beat, her nervous system short-circuited and her knees decided to wobble just a little. The sound of his dependable, powerful gait moved through her like a favorite piece of music she looked forward to hearing. She glanced over her shoulder as the big, wide-shouldered cattle rancher moseyed down the aisle.

My, he was handsome. His good looks struck her every time, renewing her hopeless crush on the man. His face was too rugged to be described as classically handsome, but she couldn't think of a single male movie lead who had aged as gracefully or as attractively as Frank Granger. His features were chiseled out of hard granite, but the man's character and warm personality softened lines that would otherwise be too harsh.

"Misty is a handful. I don't know what I'm going to do with her." Laughing, she leaned against the horse's neck because she wasn't entirely certain her feet would support her.

"So I see." Thick, dark hair fell over his

high forehead and brushed his collar, perpetually windblown. His striking blue eyes and the dimples cutting into his lean cheeks made half the unmarried women in White Horse County sigh dreamily. He wore a parka over a white T-shirt, which only emphasized the impressive line of his muscular shoulders. "How did your riding lesson go?"

"Great. I never dreamed there was so much to learn, but I'm enjoying the experience."

"I saw Autumn putting you and Misty through your paces. I hear you won't be boarding with us much longer." He jammed his fists into his coat pockets, bracing his feet apart, looking like a hero out of a western movie come to life.

"The contractor is finished with the stable. The fences are going up tomorrow so I can finally have Misty on the property with me." She would regret the lost opportunities of running into Frank, not that he felt the same way. At least she didn't think so. She took an unsteady breath, trying to hide the wound.

"That will be good for the two of you, to be together. Nothing like a bond with a horse. I spend every day with Rogue, and he's my best friend."

"I thought I was!" Autumn's voice rose out of the depths of the barn.

"Nope, you've been demoted." Blue eyes sparkled and his dimples made a breath-stealing appearance. "Ever since you agreed to marry the sheriff, I put you in second place. You're going to leave anyway."

"No way. Just you try and get rid of me." Autumn, slender and lovely with her light auburn hair and doe eyes, strolled into sight, leading a big black gelding by the reins.

She was a lovely young woman, about the age of a daughter Cady might have had if her life had taken a different course. Cady slipped one hand into her jacket pocket and extracted a molasses treat. Misty brightened, politely traded the cap for the goody and crunched on it happily. Cady tugged the hat back on her head, watching father and daughter. The pair interacted with ease only a lifetime of love and trust could give.

Frank was a good man and an even better dad. Anyone could see the respect his children had for him and the devotion he carried for them. He tugged on the end of his daughter's braid as she strolled by.

"Glad to see you up and riding again, darlin'."

"No bullet wound is going to stop me," she tossed over her shoulder with a sunny smile, her step never faltering. She had healed up from a serious run-in with cattle rustlers over two months ago, but Cady couldn't remember ever being so frightened as when she'd heard the news. She couldn't imagine how tough that had to have been for Frank.

"Dad, why don't you offer to trailer Misty over to her new home?" Autumn called out as she led the quarter horse out of sight, the clop of his steeled shoes like music echoing down the breezeway.

"I don't know why she's volunteering

me like that." A faint blanket of red tinted Frank's high cheekbones. "I'd be happy to do it, if you don't mind."

"Oh, I would be grateful." Was her unending affection for the man showing? Heavens, she hoped not. She did not want to be known as one of the many unmarried women in town who mooned after Frank Granger. She didn't have the best track record when it came to men and romance and, seriously, how many men were interested in a fifty-year-old bride? No, she wasn't holding any illusions. She caught sight of her hands, showing the wear of age with fine lines no lotion could erase, and slipped them quickly into her pockets.

"Then give the house a call when you're ready for Misty, and we'll go from there. How does that sound?"

"Fine."

Frank tossed her the same, one-size-fits-all grin he used for every occasion. The grin that said he was being friendly, but nothing more, before he went on his way. Horses in their stalls leaned against their gates, nickering to get his attention as he strolled by, reaching their necks and noses out, trying to catch hold of him.

Cady felt a nudge against her shoulder— Misty, getting her attention. She blushed, realizing she'd been staring after the man again. The chance for love had passed her by but apparently not the longing for it. Shaking her head at herself, she gathered up the towels and carted them to the laundry room. Since the washer was already chugging and swooshing, she dropped the load onto a pile on the tile floor and led Misty to her roomy corner stall. After a proper good-bye and a promise to return in a few days, Cady wandered down the aisle and stumbled when she caught sight of Frank, standing inside the wide doorway with his back to her.

"Cady, come look at this." He glanced over his shoulder, not surprised at all by the beat of her riding boots approaching, as if he'd been aware of her all along. He kept his voice low and deep, full of secrets. "I can't believe my eyes."

"Is that Tucker?" She sidled up to him, feeling small in his presence. No man had ever quite made her feel so feminine before. Somehow she forced her gaze away from the magnetic man and down the fall of hillside, along the tidy wooden fence line marching down the gravel lane to the two-story ranch house below.

"Tucker! Tucker!" Little Owen Baker's voice echoed across the hillside as he churned up grass on the lawn racing across it. Sierra, tall and lithe and lovely, trailed behind zipping up her winter coat as she walked. Sunshine gilded the threesome like figures in a Renaissance painting, making the ordinary moment transcendent.

"Yep." Frank jammed his fists into his coat pocket. "He's taken a shine to that little boy."

"You sound pleased."

"I am. This might lead somewhere." Frank latched his gaze onto hers directly. There was no filter in his compelling blue irises, no guard between his heart and hers, and an electric jolt thundered through her in the sweetest, most refreshing way.

Time spun backward and she forgot about her aging hands and the lines on her face. She forgot the reasons why she would never be appealing, the excuses she'd used to protect her neglected heart over the years.

She swallowed hard, realizing seconds ticked by, moments she lost herself in his gaze. Yes, her soul agreed. This could go somewhere. Although when she found her voice to answer him, it was Tucker and Sierra she spoke of. "I think it might lead someplace very good."

"I agree." He held her gaze for one endless second more, an intimate moment when she felt timeless and changed. When he broke away to stare at the trio down below, a new hope lifted through her. Maybe he was interested in her, after all.

"Best get Jack saddled up." Frank strolled into the wash of winter sunshine, looking like everything good and mighty in a man, everything she had ever dreamed of. "Guess I'll see you on Valentine's Day."

"Oh." Her bedazzled brain took a moment to shift gears. "My open house. Good. I'm glad you're attending."

"Me, too." His gaze found hers again across the growing distance. His heart felt nearer to hers as the sunshine brightened around her.

A whole new possible future opened up to her. *Cause me to hear Your loving kindness in the morning, for in You I do trust; cause me to know the way in which I should walk, for I lift up my soul to You.* Her morning Bible verse came to mind and she smiled.

Sierra hung back as Owen clung to Tucker's hand trustingly. The boy bounded along the gravel lane cutting between pastures, bordered by precise fencing on either side. She breathed in the fresh air carrying hints of pine forest, damp bunchgrass and horse, and felt instantly relaxed. The past handful of weeks had been anything but relaxing, so it was a welcome thing.

"Do you know what my doctor said, Tucker?" Owen skipped merrily, not taking his eyes from his hero. Goodness, it was a wonder he didn't trip.

"What did the doc say?" Tucker, to his credit, sounded deeply interested.

"That I healed up perfect."

"See? What did I tell you? You amazed him."

"Yep, you were right."

The wind carried their conversation to her as she followed behind, doing her best not to notice the dependable line of Tucker's wide shoulders or the powerful aura he radiated. It would be a lot easier if she could go back to seeing the carefree cowboy chasing no-toriety and dodging commitment. But that side of him was hard to see as he guided Owen around a clump of grass in the center of the lane before he tripped on it.

"Hey, Tucker. What happened to your cane?"

"Don't need it anymore." His voice alone could lull the most wary of women into trusting him. He shrugged one shoulder as he walked, slowing his long-legged pace to accommodate the little boy. "I rested just like my doctor said, and I healed up, too."

"Oh, boy. Are you gonna go back to the rodeo?"

"As soon as I finish up my physical therapy. I've been training hard." Shadows from the barn fell over the man and child as the two veered off the lane and into the shaded doorway. "Why, who do we have here? It's Cady Winslow."

"I'm on my way home, but I happened to get a peek at the sheep." Cady smiled in greeting and focused on Owen. "He let me pet him and everything."

"Really? Boy. Oh, boy!"

Sierra stepped inside the stable in time to see Owen jump up and down, clapping his hands. A cow mooed plaintively and leaned so far over the top of her gate, the wood groaned and threatened to buckle. Her big brown eyes fastened on the child. Her long pink tongue stretched out as if she were trying to catch hold of him.

"Look who is sayin' howdy to you." Tucker spoke low, but his voice was the only sound Sierra heard as the big man scooped her son into one arm, lifting him up so he could meet the cow at eye level. "Say hello to Buttercup."

"Hi, Buttercup." Her boy giggled. "She's trying to eat me!"

"No way. That's called a cow kiss."

Sierra tore her gaze from the duo, doing her best to keep hold of her senses.

"Owen is looking great." Cady hitched her designer bag higher on one slim shoulder, her gentle alto warming as she spun to watch the cow grab hold of the child's shoelaces and chew. Owen's giggle echoed sweetly in the rafters above. Cady's smile widened at the sound. "It must be a relief to be safely on this side of things. He's all right?"

"Thanks to your friend. If Doctor Stone

hadn't diagnosed him, who knows what would have happened? The hole in his heart had gone undetected all this time." She didn't know how a kindness like that could be repaid. She would never forget how Dr. Adam Stone had heard Owen breathing from across the diner, left his dinner and his own daughters to offer his opinion. He'd never charged her a dime for the diagnosis or his time, finding her one of the best pediatric heart surgeons in the country. "I can't thank him enough."

"That's what Adam does. He likes to help people. It's as simple as that." Cady patted her arm, a caring gesture, walking backward toward the fall of sunshine in the doorway. "You have a fun time. You work too hard, Sierra."

"I don't work hard enough, considering who it's for." Her words must have carried because Tucker chose that moment to glance over the top of Owen's ruffled brown hair and down the aisle. The impact of his gaze made her swallow hard, holding on to her composure. "I'm looking forward to your open house next week. On Valentine's Day."

"It seems fitting, since it's a romantic little inn." The sunshine engulfed her as gravel crunched beneath her riding boots. "Maybe you and Owen want to bring Tucker."

"Oh, don't give Owen any ideas." Sierra waved good-bye as the woman sauntered out of sight. Imagine what everyone in town would think if she and Tucker went anywhere together on Valentine's Day. She blushed at the thought. It had taken almost two full weeks for the rumors from the diner to die down.

"Buttercup, give those back." Tucker's good-natured laugh boomed down the breezeway, pulling her closer. He rescued the laces back from the cow. "She likes to untie shoes. Give her this treat, will you, so I can tie your shoes back up."

"Sure thing." Owen glowed, a picture of perfect health and happiness. He held out one hand. The cow licked his fingers before stealing the treat. It could have been a photograph with the big man kneeling before the boy in silhouette, strong and capable and kind.

Tucker's kindness got to her. It was only gratitude she felt as he rose, the laces successfully tied, and tossed his trademark megawatt grin. Dimples bracketed his smile, making him twelve times more handsome than the law should allow.

"I hope you came prepared, Sierra." His voice inflected her name, dropping down a full note, and the buttery rumble made her stomach flutter.

More feelings of gratitude, surely, she told herself. Definitely not more. She squared her shoulders, lifted her chin and smoothed the cowlick in her son's hair. "I hope you don't teach Owen too many rodeo riding secrets."

"No, I was only going to teach him two. That's not too many, is it?" Amusement softened the hard planes of his face.

"Maybe. Two might be too much." It was a

struggle to fashion her mouth into a straight, stern line. "Maybe you shouldn't teach him any at all."

"But, Mom! I gotta learn how to ride. I'm gonna mutton bust, remember?" Worry wrinkled her son's brow.

"All right, how about one secret?" Tucker chuckled with good humor. "He deserves at least that."

"Fine, but only if it's a very small one." She couldn't hold back her laughter.

"Mom!" Owen shook his head, as if he didn't know what was wrong with his mother. He looked sorely burdened, but not for long, as Sierra reached for his hand. Their bond was evident to anyone who could see. The little boy, so trusting, leaned against his mom's knee, walking beside her as if he knew she would always be there for him.

Nice. She looked amazing standing in the natural light from the roof windows overhead, as wholesome as could be in a sweatshirt and wash-worn jeans. She wore her golden hair down today, cascading curls framing her oval face and bouncing onto her slim shoulders. As Tucker put one boot in front of the other, he noticed the dark smudges beneath her eyes and the exhaustion she was trying to hide behind a light layer of makeup and a bright smile. He'd heard an earful in town over the past few weeks, people going out of their way to clue him in on Sierra's life. Right or wrong, folks in town sure liked to gossip.

Or, maybe they had figured him out. Perhaps he hadn't been able to hide his feelings as well as he'd thought. He knew she had medical bills, that she worked long hours and picked up extra shifts to make ends meet. He'd heard what she'd said to Cady, and he liked her devotion to her son. He liked her way, way too much.

"Just in time." Frank straightened up from checking the cinch and patted the red horse on the flank. "Owen. Look who is waiting for you."

"For me?" Owen froze in place, his eyes as wide as saucers. "Is that Jack? Is it?"

At the sound of his name, the gelding blew out a breath and swung his head around to size up the boy. The quarter horse was big and brawny, but his manner was gentle as he nickered low in his throat, stretched out his neck and lowered his head.

"He wants you to pet him, buddy." Tucker had a tough time keeping his voice unaffected. "Go on. He won't hurt you."

"My gramma has a horse." Proudly, no stranger to the breed, Owen tottered forward and held out his hand. Jack's velvety nostrils flared as he scented the boy, then with a snort lipped the boy's hair.

"That tickles!" Owen's glee rang like the most precious of sounds. It was good to see him well.

"Let's get you up in the saddle." Tucker scooped the kid into his arms, the sweetest weight there was, and eased him onto Jack's back.

"Mom! Look at me. I'm on Jack. Jack!" The boy looked about ready to explode with joy. "It's really Jack, one of the best roping horses there is!"

"Jack doesn't let just anyone ride him, but he likes you." Tucker ignored the hitch of pain in his leg as he guided little hands to the saddle horn.

"I love Jack!" Owen clutched the saddle horn with both hands. "Mom, look how high up I am. I'm taller than Tucker."

"I see." Sierra laid one hand on her son's knee, holding him in place, but she didn't need to worry.

Tucker had ahold of the boy, too. "I can't ride yet, the doc hasn't given me the clearance, so my dad is going to take you around the arena. What do you think of that?"

"Sure! Yeah." Owen twisted around to size up Frank Granger. "Are you gonna teach me to talk to animals, too?"

"Well, now, we'll see." Frank moseyed over to take the reins. "I just might be able to teach you a thing or two."

"All right!" Owen bounced in the saddle, as if excited beyond measure.

Tucker grinned. Easy to remember sitting on the back of a horse for the first time. He'd been two years old and it was a moment that had seared itself in his memory. The brisk spring wind in his face, the live, thrilling feeling of the horse shifting beneath him and the security of Dad's strong arms around him, holding him safe. He'd felt as if no force in the world could hurt him as long as Frank Granger was there.

It was still easy to feel that way. Dad talked with the little boy, who chattered right back. Owen gazed up with awe at the man mounting up and settling in the saddle behind him. Frank took the time to explain the reins and how to hold them and Owen took the leather straps with reverence.

"Now hold on," Dad advised with a wink, and Jack stepped forward down the aisle with a steady gait, as if he knew full well the precious cargo he carried in that saddle.

The little boy's delight was the happiest sound Tucker had heard in a long time. The joyful notes dug deep into him, in places he didn't know he had, touching parts of his spirit he'd rather not acknowledge. Just as he didn't want to examine what he felt for the woman who watched the horse and riders leave her sight as if her world were ending.

Sierra. He did not know what he was going to do about his feelings for her. Ignoring them would probably be the best choice, but his accident had changed him. He was no longer the man he used to be, so he didn't shove aside the awareness that came to life in those hidden chambers of his heart. He didn't push her away.

He held out his hand, unafraid. "Come with me," he said.

Chapter Eight

Sierra stared at his outstretched hand and swallowed past the lump in her throat. It had been weeks since she'd last seen Tucker in the diner, certainly time enough for the feelings he'd unearthed to settle and cool. But the instant she slipped her palm against his and felt his fingers lace with hers, gentle emotions tugged to life within her. It was as if she and Tucker had never been apart.

Perhaps this was what happened whenever two people went through something emotional together. A tie was forged that could not be broken. The closeness she'd felt and the gratitude for his kindness the morning of

Owen's surgery had forever changed things between them. But that was in the past, it had been a moment in time and nothing more. Their paths in life would always be separate. She knew that, too.

"Judging by those squeals of glee, Owen is getting a kick out of riding Jack." Tucker's easygoing manner matched his casual grin. He strolled beside her, doing his best to hide the hitch in his stride. Probably too macho to let any weakness show.

She shook her head, focused on the clean-swept concrete floor stretching before her and the echoing lilt of her son's laughter. "He hardly lets the toy horse you gave him out of his sight. It has to be in the same room with him. As for Slayer, I convinced him to leave the stuffed animal in the car, otherwise he carries it everywhere."

"I'm glad Slayer was such a hit."

"Slayer has given Owen a lot of comfort, and I'm grateful to him." She couldn't quite bring herself to let Tucker know how much his thoughtfulness meant to her, because there was always the chance her feelings would show through too honestly. Tucker was the kind of man who was probably used to women throwing themselves at him right and left. She did not want him to think she was starting to admire him, too.

"Slayer is great that way," Tucker said. "Truth is, I'm envious. I didn't get a stuffed toy when I was in the hospital." Dimples deepened, as if to hide the genuine, unspoken emotions beneath.

"Poor you." She laughed. She couldn't help herself. The man had charm to spare.

"Yep, poor me." He chuckled, as if he didn't mean a word of it and led the way into the arena. "You and Owen should stay for supper. Mrs. Gunderson did a little investigative work and found out Owen's favorite homemade meal."

"Macaroni and cheese, and barbecued hot dogs?"

"That's an affirmative."

"I can't believe you went to so much trouble for Owen."

"Truth is, it wasn't only for him." The dimples faded along with his grin, but the sincere emotions stayed as he led the way down the aisle. "I can't imagine how hard these last few weeks have been for you."

"For me? I'm not the one recovering from surgery." The arena spread out before her, a huge domed ring with fresh loam at her feet and sunshine streaming through skylights above. Owen had control of the reins, talking excitedly to Frank, who held him safely in the saddle. Oh, it was good to see her child happy. "Any other mother would have done as much. In fact, other moms might have done a better job."

"Not true. I know this for a fact." He leaned against the railing with his forearms, keeping her hand linked with his. His sadness was palpable. "Not all moms rise to the challenge."

His hadn't—she remembered the story well. Everyone in town knew how Lainie Granger had left her family without warning to live with a man in Jackson. A terrible scandal at the time, and painful for the Granger family. Sierra wished she knew what to say.

"Oh, don't look at me like that. I got over it. My brother and sisters have made their peace, too. It's my dad I worry about." He gestured toward the ring where his father sat straight and mighty in the saddle, stronger for the kindness he showed the small child in his care. Tucker's brows furrowed. "It hurt him deep."

"He's never remarried. Much to the sadness of the single ladies in this town. I hear them talking about him in the diner. It's hard not to overhear."

"One of those ladies wouldn't happen to be Cady Winslow, would it?" That thought put the smile back on his face.

"Actually, no. I've never heard her gush on about him the way Sandi Walters does. Or Arlene Miller. She's the worst. You would think a movie star strolled into the diner whenever she sees Frank walking in the door." She tilted her head to one side, lost in thought, rich blond hair tumbling over her shoulder. "Although, come to think of it, I may have caught a longing look a few times from Cady. I'll have to pay better attention."

"Take notes and get back to me. I think they've got something going on." And about time, too. Dad deserved to be happy. So did Sierra. "Think you will ever marry again?"

"Me?" Startled, she jumped back. If he hadn't had a good hold on her, her hand would have broken away from his. She shook her head hard enough to scatter her light-filled hair. "No. That is not on my agenda. One disastrous relationship has been more than enough."

She probably thought she was hiding her pain, but not from him. He could feel it like a current tugging at him, carrying him along with the power of her emotions. He didn't run from it. He didn't push it away.

He straightened his spine, set his shoulders and stepped up to the challenge. "How do you know another relationship would end up the same?"

"I don't, but I have Owen to consider." There was no hiding the devotion that transformed her as she fastened her gaze on her son. He and Frank were learning to post, Jack obligingly trotting slow and steady for the boy's benefit.

"I *can* do it!" Owen's shout echoed overhead.

Sierra lit from within as she watched her child. "I couldn't put Owen through that a second time. His heart is too much to risk."

"Yes, it is." That was his answer to a question he hadn't even formulated in his mind, much less dared to ask. He wasn't disappointed, was he? He wasn't sure what had settled heavy and pinched in his chest. "Owen is a great kid. If he were mine, I'd protect him with my life."

"Oh, says the confirmed bachelor."

"I know, easy to say, harder to do, but it's true." He made sure she couldn't see the sense of loss on his face, loss over too many things to try and figure out. Jack paraded by in a gentle cantor.

"Look at me, Mom! Look!" Owen held on with both hands to the saddle now, learning to keep his seat on a moving animal. He would need that when he met up with the sheep. "I'm ridin' Jack!"

"What a good job. Yay!" She applauded and cheered. "Go, cowboy!"

"That's me. I'm a rodeo rider!"

Thank you for this day, Lord. Never had she felt more grateful than to see Owen well and happy. She was truly blessed, indeed, and she would not forget it. The sun chose that moment to brighten, as if heaven understood.

"That's the way I learned to ride." Tucker gestured toward his father, the boy and horse as they slowed to a jouncing trot. "I remember what that was like, so excited I was about to burst at the seams, scared because that was a long way down. Most of all I felt safe because my dad was there, someone who would never let me fall. I wish I could be in that saddle today. Some traditions should be passed on."

"I didn't know you were so traditional." It was difficult to keep her pulse from picking up an extra beat as Tucker's hold on her hand tightened in a squeeze of meaning. When he released her, her palm felt cold, her fingers strangely disconnected as if she were now no longer complete.

"I'm full of surprises." He grinned his signature, coma-inducing smile and pushed away from the rail, leaving her alone. He padded over to the small rise of bleachers and pulled something off a bench. "Hey, Owen! You're not a true rodeo rider until you have your own hat."

"Oh boy!" Owen slid off the saddle and into Frank's waiting hands. The older man lowered him gently to the ground. Soft dirt rose up in puffs as the boy ran as fast as he could. "My own hat!"

"A genuine Stetson." Tucker hopped over

the low rail and knelt in the loam, hat in hand. "It's just like mine."

"It is." Owen hopped up and down in place, unable to contain his excitement as the hat settled on his head. "We match!"

"That we do, little buddy."

She wouldn't call the emotion that ebbed to life within her affection, but the quiet reverence filling her chest was definitely more powerful than gratitude. It made her see Tucker in a whole new light.

"Owen, time to meet your match." Tucker gave the boy a pat on the shoulder, gently turning him around. "That's my sister Autumn. She's bringing in Cotton Ball."

"Cotton Ball?" Owen didn't sound too impressed. He didn't blame the kid. No true cowboy wanted to think his nemesis was soft and cuddly.

"Don't let the name fool you. Cotton is a terror in disguise. A real wolf in sheep's clothing." He said that for Sierra, who watched him from the rail. He was rewarded by her rippling chuckle as Autumn led the fluffy white sheep into the ring.

"I can't believe you said that."

"Hey, I'm a cowboy, not a comedian." He liked making her laugh. She lit up from the inside, radiant with a beauty that took his breath away. For a second he forgot where he was as she swished a lock of hair behind her shoulder and her gray irises glimmered almost blue.

"You are definitely not as funny as you think." She leaned against the rail. She was picture perfect with her cheeks rosy and her smile sparkling with happiness. "Cotton does look like a toughie."

"He gave me some attitude this morning when I cleaned his stall." He knelt, wanting to look at the boy and gauge his emotions. Was Owen a little afraid and in need of reassurance? He'd gone unusually quiet. "I think he'll be a tough ride. Only the best cowboy can handle him. What do you think about that, buddy?"

"I don't wanna do a bad job." Owen took

a wobbly breath, squaring his shoulders like a determined little man. "My mom'll be disappointed."

"I don't think you have to worry about that because I'm going to help you. Come on." Tucker took the first step and waited patiently for the child to follow. "First we're going to meet him and I'll help you along. Deal?"

"Deal." Owen plodded forward, eyes wide and focused on the sheep.

Across the arena Cotton faced toward them, full of attitude. His big, friendly gaze quickly searched for any sign of a treat. Cotton was no dummy. He lifted his nose to scent the air the instant Tucker slipped his hand into his jacket pocket. A baleful "baaaah" had to be lambspeak for "hand over the treat, buddy."

"Look how big he is." Tucker pressed a molasses goody into Owen's palm. "He's a real dangerous beast. I'd be careful if I were you."

"I'm gonna look him in the eye just like you did with Slayer."

"Good. Hold out the treat for him. No need to be scared. He's ferocious, but he's basically a nice sheep." Tucker could feel Sierra's amusement wafting his way. He glanced over the top of the boy's Stetson to see her hiding her laughter behind her hands. Glad she was enjoying the show. He sent her a wink, ignored the zing of satisfaction when she winked back. Joyous, he hunkered back down to dole out more advice. "Be sure and talk to him. Introduce yourself good and proper."

"Nice to meet you, Cotton." The boy stood his ground as the animal spotted the goody, zeroed in like a nuclear submarine on a target and charged.

Dirt flew, and the sheep gained speed. Autumn ran beside the creature and choked on laughter as the fluffy beast skidded to a last-minute stop, snatched the prize from the boy's hand and crunched happily.

"My name is Owen. I want to be your

friend." He patted the sheep on his head. The animal bumped up into the stroke, the pampered pet that he was, and fastened his gaze on Tucker's coat pocket, hoping for more treats.

"Mom! Did you see? I tamed Cotton!"

"You sure did." She applauded. "Good job."

"I know." Owen seemed pleased with himself as he gave his adversary one more pat.

"Look how he's sizing you up." Tucker handed over another treat and took the lead rope from Autumn, who was doing her best to hold in her laughter.

"Too cute," she whispered.

That the boy was. Not that he was fond of him, or anything. And his mother—she represented a whole new level of fondness. It was the emotional equivalent of getting his boots stuck in the mud. He couldn't step back and he couldn't step forward and he was standing ankle-deep somewhere he didn't want to be. His gaze zoomed to her of its own will. He'd thought her beautiful in the hospital, but here in the wash of sunlight with the heavy burden of worry off her shoulders and laughter enlivening her, she looked like his heart's desire.

Strange, since he didn't know his heart had wished for anything, aside from keeping things easy and light. But there it was, his truest wish revealed.

"Do you think you can ride that wild beast?" Dad's voice boomed from the doorway as he strode back in.

Tucker, kneeling beside Owen, recalled when his father had been larger than life, a giant to the little boy he'd been, and still one to him today. Frank gentled his gruff baritone for the boy's sake, just as he'd done for his own kids. Tucker remembered that, too.

Frank knelt to give Cotton a pat. "There, there, fella. You give Owen a great ride, okay?"

The sheep let out an agreeable "baaaah,"

turning to search Frank's pockets, hoping for another treat.

Tucker laughed. He couldn't help it. Life felt right for the first time in a long while. He'd simply been drifting and he'd found his anchor. "We'll take that as an affirmative. C'mon, Owen, time to mount up."

"All right!" Excited and a little scared too, the boy gulped and straightened his spine. "Let's do this."

A perfect imitation of himself, Tucker realized, hearing what he often said before the gate opened. He felt the pull of Sierra's gaze and, as he swept Owen up into the air, he turned toward her. Time skidded to a halt when their eyes met. Dad's low-toned conversation with Owen silenced and the sun faded until there was only her.

Time did not seem to stand still for her. "Don't let him fall too hard," she said, mouthing the words so Owen would not hear.

"I won't. Promise." He'd been up early

preparing. The loam was thick and fresh, as soft as could be.

Regard chased the smile from her face. For a moment, he could not move. His pulse forgot to beat. All that mattered was the esteem he felt in the silent, shared moment.

"Tucker! I'm good to go." Owen's excitement came as if through a tunnel, drawing him back to reality.

He shook his head, trying to scatter the effects the woman had on him. It didn't work—they remained like set concrete. Normally that might panic him, but not this time. Not with Sierra. He knelt down beside the sheep, who was fidgeting, not at all sure what a little boy was doing on his back. Frank knelt on the other side of the animal, holding him in place.

"Remember what I showed you on Jack," Dad told the kid. "Hold on with your arms and your knees. Keep your head low."

"Don't forget the most important part."

Tucker tugged on the brim of the boy's Stetson.

"What's that?" Worried he'd forgotten something, those blue eyes widened.

"Have fun." He caught his dad's nod. The moment Frank released his hold on the sheep, Tucker tapped Cotton lightly on the backside. The animal hopped forward, running on his little sheep's legs. Nothing was cuter than the boy stretched out on the creature's fuzzy white back, slipping and sliding.

"Hold on, buddy!" Tucker called, straightening up to watch the progress as Cotton shot toward the center of the arena.

"That's right, Owen." Frank encouraged. "Good job. Use your knees."

The boy slid sideways, Cotton was alarmed by this and took off at a dead run. Owen went airborne and tumbled into the soft loam like a cowboy champion.

"Good ride!" Tucker clapped, dashing over as fast as he could go. The boy shoved up out of the dirt, a smile splitting his round face.

"Oh boy! Did you see me? Did you?"

"I saw, buddy. That was the best ride I've ever seen." He helped the boy up and dusted him off, hat and all. "Are you ready for another run?"

"Yeah!" Owen danced with excitement. "I can do better this time. Mom, I'm a real rodeo rider!"

"You are. The best ever." She punched the air, blond hair bouncing, a vision in a jacket and jeans. "Go, Owen. Yay!"

"Excellent ride!" Autumn chimed in with a whistle. "You did better than Tucker on his first mutton ride."

"I did?" Thrilled, Owen hopped up and down. "Is that true, Tucker?"

"I don't know. What do you think, Justin?" His older brother had moseyed in from the stables to watch the goings-on.

"Owen is definitely much better than you ever were." Justin's tone radiated great deliberation.

"I agree. Owen, that was one perfect ride." Dad had caught the sheep. "Cotton is ready to go."

"Yippee." Owen exchanged a few words with Cotton before Frank lifted him onto the back of the animal and let go.

Tucker planted his hands on his hips and joined the cheering and applauding as Owen clung to a running Cotton. Funny how life had a way of turning on you, taking you back to a place you were once sure you'd never be. He was home and happier than he remembered being.

A man's heart plans his way, but the Lord directs his steps. The Bible verse came to him as a gentle reminder that maybe this was where he'd been heading all along.

Owen hit the dirt and bounded to his feet. "Again! I gotta do that again."

Tucker felt her gaze like a touch. When he turned around, Sierra watched him with a plain gratitude that ran ocean deep.

Gratitude wasn't what he wanted from her. He had the feeling it was about all he would ever get.

Her words came back to him like a whisper from his soul. *I couldn't put Owen through that a second time. His heart is too much to risk.*

Romance wasn't in Sierra's plans. Good thing, he thought as he caught Cotton by the halter. Because romance wasn't in his plans either. Feelings were only feelings. They didn't need to go anywhere.

Across the arena, Sierra didn't take her gaze off her son. Her love and devotion radiated pure and bright, an infinite light that Tucker appreciated and admired.

Cotton searched his pockets for a treat as Owen scampered up, breathless and laughing. Good to see. He gave the sheep a pat. "Are you having fun, buddy?" Tucker asked Owen.

"Lots and lots!"

"Are you up for another run?"

"You know it!"

Cute. Tucker gave the boy's brim a tug. His gaze shot straight to Sierra. It was impossible to ignore the pangs of longing for something he'd never known he wanted before.

Chapter Nine

❧

"Owen looks like he's found paradise." Autumn joined Sierra at the family-room window in the Granger's house and handed her a cup of herbal tea. The sweet, minty goodness lifted with the steam, scenting the air.

"I don't think his feet have touched the ground once since we got out of the car in your driveway." She took the cup and saucer with thanks, not quite able to take her gaze away from the sight of her son hopping down from the two-ton truck he and Tucker had taken to haul feed to the field animals. Even far away she could read the glow as Owen tipped back his head to gaze up at his hero. He eagerly tucked his little hand in Tucker's much larger one.

"It's good to see Tucker up and about again." Rori, Justin's wife, joined them at the window with a plate of oatmeal cookies just out of the oven. "He had a hard time for a while there."

"Not that he would admit it." Autumn took a cookie. "He made light of the whole thing, but we almost lost him. I'll never forget seeing the paramedics perform CPR. He was bedridden for a month."

"You wouldn't know it to look at him now." The mother in Sierra thought cookies might spoil her supper, but the girl in her was already reaching for one. It also gave her a reason not to watch the drop-dead gorgeous man strolling down the hillside with her son. She bit into the warm, crumbly goodness, unable to keep her gaze from returning to Tucker.

"No, Tucker doesn't let anything keep him down for long." Rori bit into a cookie, too. She was tall and willowy, elegance in a sweatshirt and blue jeans. Her straight, blond hair was pulled back in a French braid. Her deep blue eyes searched the hillside until she found her husband, forking hay into a field feeder. Infinite love shone on her heart-shaped face. Married life for her and Justin had proven to be a true happily-ever-after.

It was nice to see.

"He'll be back on the rodeo circuit soon and we'll hardly see hide or hair of him again." Autumn's engagement ring sparkled in the fading evening light. "He'll probably fly in at the last moment for my wedding this June and swoop right out that night, just like he did when you married Justin."

"You know it," Rori agreed sympathetically. "You could hog-tie him, the way you always threaten."

"I may have to." Autumn chuckled at the inside joke. "I've never actually roped him down, but there is always a first time. Sierra, maybe you could persuade him to hang around. He seems to like you."

"I think it's Owen he likes." That was a nice dodge, she thought as she took a second bite of cookie.

"That's true," Autumn agreed, and Rori seconded it with an emphatic nod.

Owen spotted her in the window and waved excitedly, radiating nonstop energy. Thank God for that. The big man at his side waved, too. She felt the impact of his gaze like arrows finding their target. Her stomach quivered. She would have to come to terms with her emotions sooner or later—maybe later would be safest.

Both man and boy disappeared from sight, but their boots hammered out a rhythm on the steps and across the porch. The back door whooshed open with a gust of cool wind and voices. Owen chattered away, asking rapid-fire questions that Tucker answered with good humor and a chuckle or two.

She polished off the cookie and sipped her delicious tea, preparing for the sight of him. She didn't know what the binding connection was she felt with Tucker, but it strengthened when he sauntered into the room, stealing all the light and oxygen. She couldn't seem to draw air. No one else around her had that problem. Autumn greeted her brother with a question about one of the cows. Rori encouraged Tucker to sit down and put his injured leg up to rest, which he declined. Owen danced across the room, relaying all the excitement of helping the Granger men feed the animals and muck out barns.

"I think I hear someone coming up the driveway." Autumn spun away, abandoning her teacup and cookie. "Do you know who that is, Owen?"

"No. Who?" He clasped his hands together.

"The town sheriff. You know Ford, don't you?" Autumn held out her hand for the boy to take.

He did. "You mean Sheriff Sherman? He comes into the diner lots. He gave me and Mom a ride to the hospital, when I was real sick. He's our friend, too."

"So I heard. Let's go greet him at the door. Okay? He might let you play with his lights and siren."

"Oh, wow. Okay." Owen took two steps before he froze and glanced over his shoulder at his hero. "Can Tucker come, too?"

"Let me sit this one out, buddy." Tucker ruffled the boy's hair. "You can come find me in a bit. I've volunteered for grill duty."

"Cool." Owen tripped away with Autumn. The cheerful beat of his gait echoed in the expansive room.

"Speaking of men, I've got to go find mine." Rori sweetly excused herself, weaving around the furniture. "Tucker, I trust you can keep Sierra company."

"I wouldn't trust me with anything," he quipped and raked one hand through his thick, dark locks, standing them up on end.

Had he always been that tall? He dominated her view, overshadowed the room and made the rest of the world fade away. Mrs.

Gunderson working away in the kitchen vanished from Sierra's vision, along with everything and everyone else, leaving Tucker in the center. He gave his belt a hitch.

"I'm proud of you." Kindness rang in the low notes of his voice. "You didn't wince once when Owen hit the dirt."

"I promised myself I wouldn't be overprotective."

"After what you went through with him, that has to be tough." He must have polished those dimples just for her. She'd never seen them so dazzling.

She was about to lose her guard and defenses against him at any moment. She steeled her spine and dug deep for strength, determined to hold on. "I find myself hovering over him, worrying about every little thing."

"You don't want him to look at your behavior and think he should worry, too."

"Yes." It touched her that he understood. That a man like Tucker, a carefree bachelor with a rambling lifestyle, could empathize.

Then again, she was sure he wasn't as foot-loose as he liked to seem. "Thanks to you, I now have to worry about him growing up to ride broncs and bulls."

"You're welcome."

Why was she laughing? Because he was. His infectious, thunder-like chuckle was irresistible. "I wasn't thanking you."

"I know, but I couldn't resist." He nodded toward the door in a silent invitation and when she nodded, he settled his hand on her shoulder, guiding her along. His touch was light, a man who made no claim. "I had a blast hanging out with Owen. I learned a thing or two."

"About what?"

"It's about you." He grabbed two packages of hot dogs the housekeeper had left on the kitchen island for him. "Thanks, Mrs. Gunderson."

"You make sure and heat them clear through." The older lady looked up from dicing tomatoes with a motherly air. "I've got the coals ready. Don't burn the hot dogs."

"Relax. I am the grill master."

Sierra grabbed her coat from the row of hooks by the back door. "Does your ego know any bounds?"

"Why would you say something like that?" Spoken innocently, as if he didn't have the slightest clue.

Amusing. "First you're the best rodeo champion there is. Now you're master of the grills."

"I don't remember saying that exactly. I believe the problem is your interpretation. That tells me something about you."

"It does?" She gasped when he stole her coat from her. He seemed ten feet tall as he sidled up and held her left sleeve for her. Her stomach flipped over at his nearness, at the scents of winter wind and alfalfa clinging to his clothes. His knuckles grazed her nape as she fit her other arm into the sleeve, and tiny tingles danced all the way down to her toes. The innocent sensation filled her up until it hurt to breathe.

He didn't move away, but stayed close, gathering her long hair in his hands and gently tugging it out of the coat's collar. It cascaded free over her shoulders and he swept a wayward lock from her eyes. The brush of his fingertips against her temple shocked her because it didn't feel wrong. It was the gentlest touch she'd known.

"You don't dislike me anymore." He moved away to snare his jacket off a hook and throw it on. "Admit it."

"Impossible, since it's not true. I dislike you very much. More than ever."

"Good. I feel exactly the same way about you." With a grin hooking the corners of his mouth, he grabbed the packages of hot dogs and opened the door.

Her defenses tumbled. She stumbled outdoors as the last dregs of daylight wrestled bold colors from the sky. "I guess there's no way to stop it now."

"I've thought about it long and hard and

you're right." His boots knelled slow and
steady on the porch boards. "I have run out
of excuses. How about you?"

"Yes. Every one."

"Then I guess we have to admit it. We're
friends."

"I never thought I would see the day." She
leaned against the porch rail, gazing out at
the dusky shadows painting the hillsides.
"Remember how you used to tug on my
ponytails?"

"I remember." The barbecue lid clunked
as he set it aside. The fire licked upward,
sending smoke and heat into his face. He
popped the first pack of franks on the grill
and spread them out with a pair of tongs.

"Nearly every day for all of first grade.
By third grade it was once a week. By
sixth—"

"Once a month or so. I got better at con-
trolling myself." He remembered the bounce
and pitch of the bus as it rolled down country roads. Sierra had been such a quiet girl,

neat and tidy, doing her homework or, more often than not, reading a library book.

"It drove me crazy." Her alto strengthened. "I would keep watch out of the corner of my eye for you."

"I know. I was watching you. The minute you went into your book or a math problem, my hand would reach out. I was a menace." More like a boy who wanted her attention, not that he would ever have admitted it at the time. Or now. "You have no idea how many times I held back."

"I don't know how you ever turned out as well as you did." She leaned the small of her back against the porch rail, making a pretty picture with the background of rose-kissed fields and mauve-bellied clouds hovering in a twilight sky. She looked nothing like that introverted girl, as quiet as a mouse, and yet she was the same gentle spirit.

His heart cinched up hard. He ripped open the second pack of meat and tipped the franks onto the grill. "How did you wind up married to Ricky anyway? When Dad told me about the wedding announcement, I nearly fell off my chair."

"As you fall off things for a living, that's not saying much." Her mirth dropped away and her brightness dimmed. The shadows around her lengthened as she dipped her head, staring at the toes of her shoes instead of at him. Her long hair curtained her face. "After graduation, Ricky started being more active in the church. He became more serious. He had to ask me out at least six times before I said yes. He had never been the serious kind of guy in high school, but he was a few years older than me and he seemed ready to settle down."

"So you finally said yes." He grabbed the tongs and began rolling the franks. Sierra might have thought he wasn't watching her, but he was. He caught her small intake of breath and the way she tensed. Her hands closed into fists.

"He was very charming and I believed him. I believed in him." No trace of pain showed in her voice, but it had to be there.

She blew a strand of hair out of her eyes. "Looking back, I think he wanted to grow up and take on responsibility. But wanting something and actually doing it are two different things."

"He let you down." It didn't take a rocket scientist to figure that out, but he had to say the words. He had to hear them because he knew what she was thinking. A leopard doesn't change his spots. A man looking for the easy road would always take the fastest way out when things got tough. Tucker hated to think she might be comparing him to Ricky Baker. He moved the tongs to the second row of hot dogs and kept turning. "I'm sorry you had to go through that."

"It was partly my doing, too. I have to take responsibility." She sounded strong, like a woman who could take any wound, any catastrophe, any disappointment and let it glance right off her.

But the sun chose that moment to lose its battle with the night, and the shadows claimed her. There was nothing but her silence, nothing except her shadow lost in the dark, and in that moment of stillness he felt the whole of her. As if his heart were no longer his own, he knew how deeply she'd been hurt and how hard she'd tried to make it work. Without a single word, he knew.

"I chose poorly. Maybe I had stars in my eyes. Maybe love makes you blind and that's excuse enough. I don't know." She shrugged, a single movement in the darkness. "But if I hadn't married Ricky, then I wouldn't have Owen. And that little boy is worth everything."

He saw that, too. He'd done his best all afternoon to keep his distance from her. After the mutton busting, Cotton had retired to a comfortable stall and Tucker had taken Owen out on the afternoon rounds far away from Sierra. Bless his sister for hauling the woman back to the house where they talked about who-knew-what—probably wedding plans. It was Autumn's favorite topic of conversation lately, and rightly so. But the separation had given him a reprieve from the overwhelming pressure building in his chest, a pressure renewing in strength as Sierra gave a little sigh, an endearing sound that drew him one step closer.

"What about you?" Her words surprised him. "Why haven't you charmed some woman into marrying you and doing all your cooking?"

"Because I can cook for myself." Another step.

"I would have to see it to believe it." Mesmerizing humor dazzled in her words along with a hint of challenge, a pitch of an unspoken wish.

He took one more step nearer. "Are you trying to get me to cook dinner for you?"

"No. I would never want to risk food poisoning." Laughter lilted like a beacon in the dark, pulling him closer to her against his will.

"You're doubting me. My ego is fragile—"

"Sure it is," she scoffed.

He laughed, too. "Fine, my ego isn't frail but I can't have my reputation tarnished like this. I'm a rodeo champion. When someone throws down the gauntlet I rise to the occasion and prove myself."

"I didn't throw down a gauntlet."

"Sure you did." Humor bound them together, lifting on the wind like spring come early, chasing away every hint of cold and easing the dark.

He could see her silhouette, the willowy shape of her, the cut of her cheek, the tangle of her hair. He didn't know what made him reach out and cross the few feet separating them, but the distance was no longer safe, no longer a barrier to keep them apart. It felt as if nothing was powerful enough to do that. He reached out and her hair rasped against his fingers like fine satin, fragrant with the fruity scent of shampoo.

Tenderness seized him. He'd never felt anything like it before, powerful enough to drown him. His hand trembled as he folded a lock of hair behind her ear. Nothing he had faced in his life was as terrifying as this moment. Charging bulls or bucking broncs had never triggered this kind of terror, but he didn't back down. This woman was one hundred percent hazard to his heart.

"You can't say no now." He kept it breezy, although it took effort to produce a dimple or two. He didn't want to reveal his feelings. "I have to come over and fix dinner for Owen."

"For Owen?" She arched one delicate brow, too smart to be taken in by his charm.

But a man had to try anyway. He chuckled, the rumble intimate and nothing like the light note he was trying to strike. "Yep, for Owen. You don't want to let him down, do you?"

"He knows nothing about this offer of yours, so he can't be disappointed if I say no." She hiked up her chin. Mystery glittered in her luminous eyes.

"I don't back down from a challenge." He leaned in, closing the gap between them. The tip of his nose nearly bumped hers as his gaze intensified. "I feel an obligation to cook for Owen. I make the best spaghetti and meatballs this side of the county."

"The county?" She couldn't seem to catch her breath. Her voice came out airless and strangely affected. Could he tell? She swallowed hard and tried again. "Now you are back to bragging."

"How do you know? Maybe I'm telling the truth." Pure trouble flickered in his lapis-blue irises. "You have to let me into your kitchen to find out."

"No, I don't. Like I want a man in my kitchen." She rolled her eyes, desperately clutching humor to drive away the serious emotions rising up against her will. What had happened to her willpower? He'd shattered every last defense, forcing her to stand before him with her heart exposed. Could he see?

"Hey, I'm not any man." His humor fell short, and seriousness settled between them.

Her midsection twisted up. She wasn't

comfortable with seriousness, so she had no choice but to fight it. She cleared her throat, pitched her voice up a note and did her best to smile wide. "There you go with the ego again."

"It's not ego. It's fact." He tilted in, his mouth hovering over hers.

"Fact?" A chuckle escaped her—it was her only resort. She was trapped between the wooden porch railing and Tucker's unyielding frame. He towered over her; he was all she could see. Her vision had adjusted to the deepening twilight and she could make out the solemn gleam in his gaze, the fierce set of his granite face, the shape of his lips as they hovered over hers. Every detail etched into her mind, a moment in time forever frozen and impossible to forget.

"I broke my collarbone trying to ride a green horse when I was fourteen."

Her pulse screeched to a stop. They were kissing-close, but he did not move in to claim her. His bottom lip whispered against hers every time he formed a word. Did she move away? Did she give him a shove to escape?

Not a chance. She stood rooted to the ground, her hands glued to the wooden banister. Every neuron in her brain refused to fire.

"Aunt Opal was none too pleased with me," he explained in hushed, intimate tones. "She could see the way of things. I had the rodeo bug and she didn't approve."

"A wise woman wouldn't."

"Exactly. She said if I was fool enough to hurt myself, I deserved to help out in the house since I couldn't do my barn chores. She put me to work in the kitchen." Tantalizing, the way his mouth nudged against hers.

The contact was sensational, like the joyful hues at sunset. The sensations rushing through her were quiet and reverent, like the tints of low light at dawn. She leaned into the sweetness and illumination of her feelings, realizing that she was also physically leaning toward him, and the brush of his lips to hers became a gentle pressure that did not fade. The joy within her brightened and the reverence crescendoed like a hymn's chorus.

At the back of her head, her thoughts raced. I'm kissing Tucker Granger. That can't be a good thing. Have I lost my mind? But at the forefront was his tender kiss, so chaste and respectful, he captured her.

The porch light flipped on, chasing away the disguising dark. Regret shadowed Tucker's gaze as he broke away. The screen door swung open with a squeak.

"How are the hot dogs coming along?" Frank Granger stood in the doorway grinning widely, as if he'd witnessed the whole thing. "I've got a houseful of hungry folks waiting."

"They're probably done by now," Tucker answered, and not even the flash of his dimples could chase away the ardent tenderness that rose within her like a song.

Chapter Ten

What a disaster. It was all she could think about during supper, seated at the big oval table in the Granger's dining room. It was all she could think about any time Tucker spoke or when her gaze drifted his way. Her mind played cruel tricks on her, replaying the innocent glory of his kiss in full, vivid Technicolor.

The kiss plagued her as she hurried into the kitchen to take charge of the dishes—no way was she giving in to everyone's insistence that a guest not help with cleanup. If not for the sanctuary of the kitchen, then she would have had to sit in the living room with Tucker and try to keep her eyes from finding him or her heart from leaping every time she heard the familiar, treasured tone of his voice.

Something is seriously wrong with you, Sierra Lynn Baker, if you can't stop thinking about that man's kiss. She wrung soapy water from a dishcloth and scrubbed the pristine granite counter.

"Easy, lass." Mrs. Gunderson straightened up after putting soap into the dishwasher. "You don't want to rub off the finish."

"Sorry." She was upset at herself, wondering what on earth Tucker had been thinking to kiss her like that. He'd kissed her! Out of the blue. Unbelievable. She really ought to be mad at him, so why wasn't she?

That was a question she was afraid to answer. She turned her attention to scrubbing a bit of dried cheese sauce from the counter, but not even cleaning could distract her. The rise and fall of Tucker's voice mumbled from the neighboring room. The roar of a crowd, the boom of commentators and Owen's excited shout told her they must be watching a rodeo—what else? She shook her head, returned to the sink and dowsed the cloth in sudsy water.

"If you want my opinion," Mrs. Gunderson said, untying her apron, "you should go for it."

"Go for what?"

"A romance with that boy. If I were forty years younger, I might beat you to it." She winked, and a smile wreathed her pleasantly round face. Gray curls bounced as she ambled across the room. "He's a good boy."

"He's a man who hasn't grown up." Sierra laid the cloth over the edge of the sink, keeping her voice low. "I've made that mistake before."

"He seems grown up to me. Then again, I've only known him since November." The housekeeper grabbed her coat and keys by the back door. "Well, just a little friendly advice."

"Good night, Mrs. Gunderson." As if

she needed advice. What she needed was a smack upside the head! Mostly because her lips continued to buzz pleasantly with the gentle memory of his kiss.

What a kiss. That was the problem. The man was extraordinarily gifted at kissing. He knew how to make a woman feel special and sweetly treasured with one single brush of his lips. How could any female resist that?

Which made it all his fault, she decided as she dried her hands on a towel hanging over the oven handle. Alone in the kitchen with only the chugging dishwasher to keep her company, she leaned to one side to get a good look into the living room. A big sectional was centered in the space and faced a large wide-screen TV. She stared at the back of Tucker's head, doing her best not to notice all his thick, tousled brown hair, not to let in a single emotion. Not one.

"Hey." As if he sensed her attention, he turned, his tone soft as velvet. The room's bright light gave color and definition to the face she'd been trying to keep in the shadows of her mind. His vivid blue gaze speared her sharply enough to make her gasp. He stood, not caring that the rest of the occupants in the room turned to watch him go.

Were they all wondering what was going on? She wrapped her arms around her middle, hating that Frank might not be the only one who had witnessed that kiss. Mrs. Gunderson might not be the only one capable of putting the pieces together.

"It's time to take Owen home." She braced herself for the reaction. Sure enough, her son hopped to his knees on the couch and stared at her over the cushions.

"Aw, Mom. Can't we stay? Tucker and me, we're watching the rodeo. It's the one where he showed Slayer who was boss."

"A taped rodeo." Not so dire, then. "You probably have the same one at home, so you can watch it later. Time to hit the road, handsome."

"Did you hear?" Owen tilted his head back

to wink at his new cohort in crime. "We can watch it later. You gotta come over."

"Will do, buddy." Tucker ambled toward her, looking mighty pleased with himself. Probably thinking he would get all sorts of kisses, that she was one of those poor, misguided women who couldn't say no to a dashing, heart-stealing cowboy.

Except she knew that wasn't true of Tucker. She wanted to keep believing it, but she couldn't. The man crooked his forefinger at her son.

"C'mon. Let's do what your mom says." *Mighty* was a word that came to mind. *Honorable* was another.

Owen's shoes hit the carpet with a thud. She ducked into the mudroom, where the coats were lined up in a row on hooks, her back to Tucker. There was no escape from him. His boots sounded steadily on the floor behind her, his hand caught her coat before she could unhook it, and he held the garment for her, dangerously close.

"Before you say it was a big mistake, let

me do it first." His confession rose and fell with an easy cadence. Nothing seemed difficult for him, not even admitting to a lapse in good judgment. "A big oops. That kiss was a complete accident."

"You *accidentally* kissed me?"

"Yep. My lips bumped into yours. Don't know how it happened."

Honestly. What was wrong with the man? Or with her, because her gaze slid down the lean lines of his face to rest on the sculpted bow of his lips. Forget the kiss, Sierra. She had to will away the memory, but it was impossible. For as long as she lived, she would remember the reverence and purity of his kiss. She shook her head, determined to cling to some semblance of common sense.

"Mom!" Owen pounded in, breathless. "Can Tucker come over tomorrow?"

"Not tomorrow." Not for a long time, if she had her way. She grabbed Owen's coat and tried not to scowl at Tucker when he beat her to it. "I work tomorrow."

"Then the day after that?" Owen pleaded as he stuck his fist into one sleeve, then the other. The big man helping the little boy into his jacket was quite a sight, one she would not let sway her stance.

"No. That's the day we go to the party at the inn." She opened the door. Night had fallen, and the country air iced her face. "Another time."

"Then how about the day after that?" Owen persevered as he trudged behind her onto the porch.

"We'll see." She reached out for his hand, but he was already holding on to Tucker's. The big man snared his coat from its hook and stepped out onto the porch, closing the door behind him, shutting out the sight of his father, brother, sister-in-law, sister and future brother-in-law, all watching curiously.

Great. Think of the rumors if she didn't nip this in the bud. Her breath rose in white puffs as she led the way down the stairs.

"That means no." Owen blew out a sigh. "She always says it doesn't, but it does."

"Leave it to me, buddy. Okay?"

"Okay." Owen's plodding step turned to a skipping one. "Thanks, Tucker."

"Don't thank me yet."

The musical cadence of his chuckle made her want to turn around, but she held firm. She followed the fall of outside floodlights around the corner of the house to the driveway, where her SUV sat in full illumination. In a nearby field, wildlife scurried away from the movement as Tucker opened the passenger door for Owen and helped him in.

An accidental kiss? He was outrageous. Against her will a giggle caught in her throat and she battled it down. Really. She opened her door and dropped into her seat. She wanted to believe that Tucker was the type of man who experienced accidental kisses all the time, but down deep she knew that wasn't true.

Tucker was a solid man like his father and his older brother. Steadfast, hardworking and honest, they were men who cared about God, family and others.

Don't make that mistake again, she warned herself as she dug her keys out of her coat pocket. Don't go finding the good in the man and ignoring the flaws. She'd done the same exact thing with Ricky. Seeing the man who wanted permanency and stability and family ties but not the responsibility, hard work and commitment that went with them. She sorted through the keys on her ring, drowning out the sound of Tucker's conversation with her son, light and humorous and resonating with something she didn't want to name.

That would be *caring*. True affection layered every word, every soft chuckle, and if she glanced into the rearview mirror, she knew she would find it stark on his lean, far-too-attractive face. The man wasn't simply being nice to her son. How was she going to keep from falling for him now?

Clueless, she turned the key, the engine came to life, music blared from the speakers and a big hand settled on her shoulder. Tucker knelt beside her, toppling every defense she was trying to build.

"I've got a confession to make." He leaned in, making the darkness seem so vast and accentuating the fact that, aside from Owen, they were alone together. Very alone. Again. Trouble lurked in his dimples. "Want to hear it?"

"No. Absolutely not." Yes, she wanted to say. She was so absolutely interested she didn't know how to hide it—if she could. She set her chin as if nothing in the world could annoy her more. "You can keep your confessions to yourself."

"I could do that, but then we have to talk about something." Trouble turned into a much bigger problem as he inched closer, exactly as he'd done right before he'd slanted his lips over hers. "The natural course of events would be to go from my confession to what you aren't confessing."

"What? I'm not sure that made any sense." Best to try to derail him from his course because where he was heading could not be good. The tremble in the pit of her stomach told her so.

"Sure, I'm making sense. You just don't want to talk about it, and I can see why." The problematic dazzle of his charm turned dangerous. "Especially since you don't want to admit the truth."

"There is no truth."

"Sure there is." The weight of his hand increased, his fingers curled around her shoulder and slid upward to the nape of her neck. "You kissed me back."

"I did no such thing!" Alarmed, she jerked toward the mirror, but Owen was busy rescuing his stuffed bull from the backseat and settling it into his arms. A complete relief he hadn't overheard that. The adrenaline in her blood made her dizzy.

"You can deny it." Tucker spoke low against her ear. "But I know it and that's what matters."

If only she could come up with exactly the right comeback, the perfect, flippant remark to stop him in his tracks. Her mind remained blank. Nothing clever or smart popped into her head. She could only stare at him, her vocabulary missing in action and her dignity gone right along with it. A smart girl would escape while she could. She gave her seat belt a yank but he took it from her, clicking it into place with a flourish. If only his deep blue eyes would flash that easy-going cowboy charisma so she could go back to the way she'd originally felt about him. Then it would be much easier to give him a push, close the door and drive away as if she wasn't the most foolish woman in the world.

Instead she felt lost in his sincere gaze, the pull of his emotions, and the glimpse of his honesty caught her like a lasso's noose.

Tenderness softened his handsome features and gave depth to the man he was. He released his hold on her, rose to full height and gripped the edge of the door. "Good night, Sierra. Drive safe."

"I will." The words stuck like peanut

butter in her throat. "Thanks for all you did for Owen today."

"It was my pleasure." Maybe it was a trick of the starlight, but he stood so tall, surrounded with stardust, grand enough to be her entire world. Shadowed, his true self shone through, his essence that the darkness could not seem to hide. Noble. Unfailing. Kind. The adjectives didn't stop but rolled into her mind, making her want to believe.

Don't do it, she told herself. She set her jaw, fighting the urge to give in. Don't make a mistake Owen will pay for. Her hands trembled as she set them on the steering wheel at the ten and two o'clock positions. She didn't dare let her gaze drift toward the man as he closed the door. The barrier of metal and glass was no defense against the awareness that telegraphed between them, like recognizing like. It did not shut out the impression he made—mighty, genuine, gallant.

He lifted one hand as they pulled away.

Although he was nothing more than a shadow against the dark fields, it felt as if she carried a part of him with her as she drove miles of country roads, ribboned through fields and rolled into the sleepy town and beyond. The tie binding them remained as she spotted the reflector on her mailbox post and pulled into her driveway.

Tucker. What was she going to do about his kiss? She didn't have the foggiest idea. They stopped beneath the shelter of the carport. Owen had fallen asleep in the backseat, so dear and darling and handsome he took her breath away.

He was her love. Her one true love. She turned off the engine, pocketed her keys and opened the door. Icy air pummeled her as she opened Owen's door. She couldn't forget this precious blessing she'd been entrusted with. Her son was her whole heart, so how was Tucker working his way in?

Lord, give me strength to resist that man. She unbuckled Owen and gathered him into her arms. Her son's eyelids fluttered. He tightened his hold on Slayer and burrowed into her shoulder. Contentment filled her as she carried him down the dark sidewalk and up the porch steps. Her footsteps whispered around her as she hit the lights and ignored the growing list of things that needed to be done—the laundry, the dusting, the bills piling on the counter—and carried her son to bed.

Poor little guy. So tired out from his big day he could barely lift his head. She stepped over a plastic barnyard scene spread out on his bedroom floor, pulled back his covers and eased him onto the flannel sheets.

"Tucker," he mumbled on a sigh and snuggled his stuffed bull tight in his arms.

She winced. Owen was getting attached to his favorite cowboy. Maybe too attached.

Not knowing what to do about it, she knelt to untie his sneakers. The glow of the day remained, a happiness she could not dowse. Her son's delight over riding Jack, his squeals of glee as he clung to Cotton's back and the way he'd stuck to Tucker's side

on the couch as they'd watched the rodeo—
these had given her great joy, too. All the
Grangers had done everything they could
to make sure Owen enjoyed his day.

She tucked the covers around him and
kissed him good-night. His flyaway hair
across his forehead tickled her nose. Unending sweetness filled her. She backed out
of the room, remembering to step over the
plastic toy barn, cows and horses.

Maybe she didn't have to worry about the
kiss. Her feelings for Tucker couldn't go
anywhere. He wasn't a man ready to settle
down. As for his relationship with Owen,
she knew after today Tucker would never
hurt her son. Their friendship was real.

Alone in the hallway, she shut her child's
door tight. She may as well be closing the
door on her heart. She had no room for
wishes other than the ones she already
had.

"Yeah, I know I'm in big trouble." Tucker
could tell by the arch of Jack's neck what

the horse thought. He eased open the stall door and sauntered in, welcoming the scent of livestock, sweet hay and alfalfa, comforting smells that always soothed him in time of need.

With a low-throated nicker, Jack trudged over, his steel shoes ringing against the floor. The gelding was sixteen hands of powerful muscle, pedigreed lines and personality. The big horse lowered his head, placed his muzzle in Tucker's hands and leaned his forehead into Tucker's chest. Another moment of comfort. They had been friends a long time. Tucker had helped deliver him, and Jack had been Dad's gift when he'd graduated high school with honors. He ran his fingers along the horse's jaw, just the way Jack liked. There wasn't a better horse anywhere on this planet. Not one.

"You did good today, buddy."

Jack lifted his head and snorted, as if he'd never questioned it. His red mane rippled in the lamplight and he looked every inch the champion he was.

"Little Owen sure loved riding you." Tucker rescued from his back pocket the paperback he'd grabbed in the tack room. "Then you wouldn't mind seeing him again?"

Jack nodded, as if in perfect agreement.

With a chuckle, Tucker rubbed the gelding's glossy neck. "I miss riding you, buddy. I miss a lot of things." The adventure, the traveling, never knowing what was around the next corner. What he liked the most about his professional life was the animals. He'd grown up with them and he couldn't imagine being without them.

When he'd woken up in ICU with the compelling feeling he'd been given a huge gift of grace, the first thing he'd seen was his father at his bedside. The haggard worry on Frank's face had said everything. Dad had stayed in the hospital with him, waiting on him hand and foot. They'd kept things light—that was their way—but in the unspoken silence he knew. He'd come close to leaving this life. Close enough that he could still remember the feeling of heavenly arms around him when he'd fallen off that horse. Heaven had been protecting him.

Lord, I know you have something in mind for me. He might not be sure what that was just yet, but he was getting an idea. His chest felt tight and bunched-up from Sierra's visit, but that wasn't a bad thing. He'd spent so much of his life running from his emotions or doing his level best to deny them. He wasn't good at looking them in the face, but he was going to try.

Footsteps ambled closer, breaking the silence in the stable. Horses woke up to whinny greetings, the noise echoing in the rafters. Tucker slid his book back into his pocket. Looked like he wouldn't get the peace and quiet to read with Jack. He braced his forearms over the gate, not surprised to see his dad moseying to a stop.

"I thought I might find you out here." Dad shrugged the strong, wide shoulders that time had not yet been able to diminish. For a man in his fifties, Frank was vital and powerful, but a hint of gray had set in at his temples. Just a hint, and it was reminder enough that time was passing.

A knot tightened in his chest until it hurt. He might enjoy his life riding bareback broncs and bulls, but a rodeo wasn't home. He missed his dad. He missed him with a yearning he couldn't explain. Not that he felt comfortable talking about it, so he stuck with what was. "I wanted to spend some time with Jack. I hate not riding him."

"Another few weeks and you'll be back in the saddle." Dad handed over an ice-cold can of root beer and kept one for himself. "It was a good thing you did today. Owen had a great time. Remember back when I borrowed Fluffy? You took one look at that sheep and thought I was ridiculous."

"I was wrong. It didn't take me long to figure that out." It had been more than twenty years ago and yet it felt like a blink. He'd been so busy running that he'd never given much thought to what he'd left behind. He was doing it now. "I wouldn't be where I am in life if it wasn't for you, Dad."

"You mean busted up and healing from too many broken bones to count?" Dad excelled at sidestepping emotional topics, too.

"That's exactly what I mean. It's all your fault." His throat tightened painfully with feelings he was too embarrassed to reveal, so he popped the top off the can and took a refreshing swig. Jack ambled over to check out the can. He wasn't fond of soda and wrinkled his nose, making a face that was hard not to laugh at.

Judging by the relief in his dad's chuckle, Frank was glad not to talk about those pesky emotions, too. So they turned the conversation to safe topics—hiring cousin Sean to help out on the ranch so Autumn could be free to prepare for her wedding and a much-deserved honeymoon, getting Cotton back to Mr. Green tomorrow and keeping an eye on the brood mare in the end stall who was getting near her time. Dad was merciful enough not to once mention Sierra or the kiss he'd no doubt witnessed.

Tucker wouldn't likely forget that kiss anytime soon. Maybe never. He could tell himself he wasn't capable of love, that in all his twenty-eight years he'd never fallen for any woman.

Thanks to Sierra, that was no longer true.

Chapter Eleven

Cady Winslow knew the moment Frank Granger stepped foot inside the inn's front door. Not one single thing changed—not the rise and fall of the conversations in the lobby surrounding her, not the crackling warmth from the fire snapping in the drawing room's stone hearth and not the crush of the well-attended open house. Butterflies settled in her stomach. Her palms went damp. Her knees tried turning to jelly.

Yes, she knew her symptoms when Frank Granger came into sight. She pivoted in her dress shoes, aching for the first look at him. Her pulse hit a staccato beat as her eyes found him. My, he was handsome. The guards protecting her heart tumbled down. The crowd vanished, her surroundings faded, except for the tall, strapping man ambling her way.

"This place is mighty fancy. Looks like something out of an upscale magazine." He didn't look right or left as he came to a stop before her. "I've got your mare outside. Figured since we were coming over, I might as well trailer her up. Autumn's putting her in the corral, if you want to go see."

"I do." When he held out his hand, palm up, her fingers landed there without thought.

It felt as natural as breathing to fall into step at his side, moving in unison with him through the crowd. Voices called out, coming as if from miles away, so distant she couldn't recognize a word or sound above the fluttering thud of her pulse in her ears. She didn't remember crossing the lobby because of the comforting security of his calloused, much larger hand enveloping hers.

When he withdrew his touch, her surroundings swam back into focus. The din of conversation returned with a surge, as if too loud to bear. The sunshine streaming through the windows burned her eyes, brighter than it had ever been.

"Here. This will keep you warm." His winter coat settled around her shoulders and he moved in close. She could hear the whisper of his breathing as he helped her with the sleeves.

"Thank you." Head spinning, knees trembling, she prayed with all her might she appeared calm and normal because it was *not* how she felt.

The door swung open and the Wiseners stormed in. Smiling proudly, Tim Senior with his mayoral stance surveyed the inn. "Hi there, Cady. What a fine place this is. Tim Junior told us all about it of course, so we knew it would be nice. But this is something else to see."

"Your son did a fine job with the renovation." Cady tried to make her brain work appropriately, but it was on overload. The only thing in focus was Frank, dark hair slightly tousled from the wind, ruggedly handsome and mighty of character.

"Cady, this is marvelous." Martha, Tim's wife, charged in, unbuttoning her coat. "I haven't seen the final touches. Very well done."

"Thank you." A shot of cool air breezed over her. Frank held the door open and her feet carried her to him of their own accord. Without thought, she was at his side, waltzing past him through the threshold and pausing to wait for him on the wide, old-fashioned porch.

"This was quite a project." His boots reverberated on the boards as he drew near. "You must be glad to see this renovation done."

"Yes, it's been a challenge, but I've loved every minute." They tapped down the wide steps together and onto the concrete walkway that rolled pleasantly toward the packed parking lot, where a florist's van was pulling in. Frank veered left and so did she.

They followed the path ribboning through the grounds. "It's a dream come true."

"You don't get too many of those in this life. Seems that when a good dream comes true, you ought to really enjoy it."

"That's my plan." She felt shy and her tongue tied up.

Frank seemed a little uncomfortable, too. He rubbed the back of his neck with one hand. "I suppose you'll be busy running this place."

"I've hired an executive manager." Relax, Cady. She took a deep breath that wound up being a very shallow one. No man had ever affected her like this. She felt inexperienced, as if the past decades of her interactions with men hadn't existed, both professional and personal—emphasis on unsuccessful interactions there. "I retired from a job working up to a hundred-hour weeks, sometimes more. I don't want to do the same thing here."

"Smart. You want to take it easier these days?"

"That's one reason I left New York." Frank had the nicest dimples, making it so hard to concentrate. She couldn't remember what she'd intended to say next. Way to go, Cady.

Frank didn't seem to notice. His gait slowed. "Then I guess you will have more free time. Maybe you might like to go out to dinner with me."

"With you?" As in a date? Her feet froze to the ground. The February sun faded and she shivered. Had her ears deceived her or had Frank Granger just asked her out?

"I understand if you want to take a pass." He shrugged his shoulders, endearingly and ruggedly self-conscious. "I've been told I'm not the best at dinner conversation. Truth is I haven't been on a date since I was nineteen. That can't be good. It would be smart to avoid me."

"I haven't been on a date in a long time either." The wind breezed against her with a gentle touch, and she no longer felt the crisp bite in the air. Gazing into his perfect blue eyes, her soul stilled. Never had she been more sure of anything in her life. "Yes. I would like to go to dinner with you."

His dimples returned to full wattage as he fell into stride beside her. "How does a week from Friday sound?"

"Great. Things should be calmed down around here by then and into a routine." Had she ever been this happy? If so, then she couldn't remember it.

They continued on. Up ahead the fresh white paint on the fence boards and new stable contrasted pleasantly with the fallow grasses. One day the corral would hold several horses for guests to ride, but only one horse stood in the field, a golden mare with a white mane, a creature so lovely it hurt the eye to see.

The mare's head shot up, she whinnied a happy greeting and raced up to the fence. Autumn strolled into sight behind the truck and trailer, followed by her two strapping brothers.

"Cady!" Autumn sailed into her arms for a

quick hug. What a sweet girl. "I think Misty likes her new digs. She's been racing around, checking everything out. We brought over her tack and some essentials. We'll get the hay unloaded in the barn."

"You shouldn't be working. I'll call to the front desk. I've hired someone to handle the horses." She reached into her pocket, doing her best to concentrate. Frank had finally asked her out. She couldn't believe the moment had been real. Did her excitement show? Could anyone tell she was jumping for joy inside?

Frank gave no sign that he felt anything of the like as he ambled up to the fence. "Hi, Misty." He rubbed the mare's nose with the ease of a man who'd been around animals all his life. The quarter horse nickered, speaking to him in her horsey way. He mumbled back, quite as if he understood everything.

The sunlight burnished his mighty physique. As impressive as he was, his kindness mesmerized her. She could not help the tumble of her heart, falling further in love with the man. He'd asked her out! She still couldn't believe it.

Her cell rang as she closed her fingers around it, so she dragged it out of her pocket and squinted at the screen. The front desk was calling. "Hello?"

"Two things." Eloise, the inn's executive manager, got right to the point. "The florist just delivered several bouquets for the guests, but there's one for you."

"For me?" That couldn't be right. "You mean for the inn."

"Nope. It has your name on the card, from someone named Frank. Two, Jonah is here and wants to ask you a few questions for the town paper."

"Tell him I'm on my way." Cady slipped the phone into her pocket, loath to leave. She sidled up to the fence to lay her hand on Misty's warm, velvet neck. The mare nickered, torn between the humans on either side of her. She let Cady pat her nose and then offered it to Frank.

"Guess you have to go?" Across Misty's forehead, his blue gaze searched hers.

It was regret she read there and something else—latent happiness. She knew because the same sparkle danced in her soul. Frank was interested in her. That was a prayer come true.

"Yes. I'll send Rocco out." She should have remembered to ask for him on the phone. "He can take care of all of this."

"I don't mind." His assurance came softly in a tone that held a hundred unspoken promises, as if this moment between them was only the beginning.

Happiness lifted her up as she gave him a little wave and turned away. It wasn't easy to leave him, but she knew he would be joining her inside soon. Her shoes didn't touch the pathway as she hurried back to the inn.

"I'm going to have to cut your hours." Darla Rogers, the diner's owner, stirred a spoonful of sugar into her coffee.

The lunch rush was gone—not that it

could accurately be called a rush, Sierra reasoned, as she fidgeted in her chair. She wasn't the only one squirming. Around the table, the other employees were attempting to cope with the news. Were they fighting a bad sense of foreboding in their stomachs, too?

"I'm keeping one waitress on per shift. Carol asked for tonight, so Sierra, you are off." Darla's shoulders slumped. "I wish things were different. Business has been slow."

Wow, not the news she needed to hear. First, don't panic. She had savings to rely on for a while—a short while. But neither had the news come as a complete surprise. With the economy, folks weren't eating out as often.

"Maybe it's just the time of year," Sandi, the cook, chimed in hopefully. "Things will pick up when the weather turns warm."

"It's the economy. It's my upcoming divorce. It's a lot of things." Darla sighed, obviously unhappy. "I need to cut your hours significantly. It's the only way to keep the doors open."

But for how long? That was the question no one dared ask. This wasn't the first time they had been in this situation. The diner had been sold or closed down more than a few times over the years. Some businesses had a hard time surviving in a small ranching town, good economy or not.

The door swung open, letting in a gust of chilly air. The sun was out, but clouds were moving in. It smelled like snow as the door banged open wide. A delivery man stumbled into the diner behind a vase of pink carnations. Several dozen blossoms bobbed amid a sprinkling of white freesia, and the fragrance was sublime. What a lovely bouquet.

"Sierra Baker?" The young man glanced toward their table, since the diner was otherwise empty.

"That's me." Confused, she shook her head. Why would he call her name?

"Then this is for you." He sauntered over.

"For me?" That couldn't be right. She didn't get flowers, not these days. Not unless Owen picked them for her. She stared in disbelief as the delivery guy set the vase on the tabletop.

"Enjoy. Happy Valentine's Day." He ambled off the way he had come, the door whooshed closed and she was left blinking at the arrangement, which apparently wasn't a figment of her imagination. It sported a card with jaunty handwriting she recognized from her school days.

"Woo-hoo!" Sandi beamed.

"I knew it." Connie clapped enthusiastically. "Tucker Granger is sweet on you, girlfriend."

"No. He can't be. Tucker?" Surely there was another explanation. A perfectly rational one, although the only one flashing into her mind was his kiss. His amazing kiss.

Why couldn't she forget that kiss? A sensible woman would drive all traces of it from her mind, delete it like a computer virus and toss it out like the enormous, gigantic, colossal mistake it was.

Even if it had been a very nice and exceedingly sweet mistake.

"No, Tucker isn't serious." She shook her head, refusing to believe it, refusing to let in the tiniest hope. "He will fly out of town as fast as he can find transportation once his leg is healed. There isn't anything keeping him here."

"Trust me." Sandi breathed in a good whiff of the fragrant blossoms. "I've known that family all my life. I've kept them under close observation. That young man is exactly like Frank. Hardworking, loyal and doesn't give his heart easily. When he does, it's for keeps."

Why did her stomach flip over? Why did hope flicker to life against her will? She stroked one pink petal with the tip of her finger. Tucker wasn't hers to keep. She didn't want to keep any man. She had Owen to protect, a living to make for him and no time to fall in love. So why did her mind spin in that direction, giving her all sorts of visions of an impossible future? Tucker riding Jack with Owen, Tucker watching rodeos with Owen, Tucker barbecuing hot dogs on her front porch for Owen.

Impossible. Images that could never come true. Why was she torturing herself like this? And worse, why was she upset at the prospect of those dreams of Tucker not coming true?

I'm not in love with him. She set her jaw, grabbed the vase and stood. The meeting might not be over, judging by the puzzled look Darla gave her, but she didn't care. She had to be upset over the loss of hours and the corresponding wages. That was why her throat felt on fire and the foreboding in her stomach had migrated to her chest. It had nothing to do with Tucker, nothing at all. At least, it gave her comfort to think it was true.

In the coatroom, she set the vase down and opened the card with her name on it. Tucker's handwriting. He'd gone to the trouble of driving over to Sunshine to order the flowers in person. She tried not to read anything into that as her eyes scanned the note.

I'll confess that kiss was no accident.

She so did not believe what Sandi had said about him being a serious man. Serious? Hardly. She could hear the humorous lilt in those words. Easier to tell herself he was simply being charming because the alternative frightened her more than she wanted to admit.

Do not fall in love with him. She slid the card into her purse, zipped up her coat and tucked the vase into the crook of her arm. As she tapped out the back door and across the parking lot, the floral scent put a spring in her step she could not seem to contain.

The sunshine dimmed as cloud cover moved in and it felt like a sign. If she lost her heart to a man she couldn't have, how foolish would that be? Monumental. She had to be firm, keep her affections hidden and refuse to acknowledge them so they would fade away.

Her SUV waited curbside on Second Street. After she stowed the vase, buckling it in so it wouldn't tip, she was at loose ends. A glance at her watch told her Mom would have already picked up Owen from day care, so she started the engine and headed home. The heat from the vents stirred the aroma from the blossoms, making it impossible to forget the man who'd sent them.

Not an accidental kiss. She gripped the wheel tighter, ambling down Second and turning right at the medical clinic. Why did he have to go and confess it? Worse, why was she missing him? Why couldn't she get the man out of her head? He'd haunted her for days and nothing could dissipate the tenderness she was beginning to feel for him or the effect of his kindness, the poetry of his kiss.

Lord, don't let me make another mistake. She wasn't sure if God could hear her. Tiny flakes of snow appeared, falling weightlessly, effortlessly on the wind. By the time she pulled into her driveway, white covered the ground, obscured the grass and highlighted the big black pickup parked in front of the door. Tucker's truck.

"Mom!" Owen bolted onto the porch, bundled up in his warmest jacket, a hat, mittens and his snow boots. Puddles bounded alongside him. "Guess what! Tucker's here."

"So I see." Sierra turned off the engine and unbuckled, aware of the man lumbering toward the carport. Don't look at him. She had to keep cool, act as if she wasn't thrilled to see him. Because she wasn't. She couldn't be. She opened her door. "Tucker's here. The question is why."

"To make the best spaghetti ever!" Owen answered, clasping his hands together. "And it smells good, too."

Puddles barked as if in perfect agreement.

"A promise is a promise." Tucker stood over her, more good-looking than ever in a simple black parka, a blue knit cap and wash-worn Levi's. The power of his gaze and the magnetism of his presence seemed to demand her attention. "Didn't I say I would come over and cook for you?"

"I don't remember agreeing to anything so suspicious."

"Suspicious?" He laughed at that, opened the back door and freed the flowers. "No need to doubt my intentions. You didn't think I could cook, so I'm here to prove it to you."

"I don't need proof. I've changed my mind. I'm willing to take you at your word." She could not keep her gaze from meeting his and the impact ricocheted all the way to her soul. Not exactly the reaction she was hoping for.

"So, you are starting to trust me. That's progress." He winked, stalking on his long, athletic legs through the tracks of snow he and Owen had made. "It's Valentine's Day, so I thought it was the perfect excuse."

"For what?" She tapped up the steps,

hardly aware of her shoes slipping on the slush.

"To see you again." He held the door open for her, so close she could see the hints of five o'clock shadow on his lean, square jaw. "Don't let the flowers fool you. I almost went with roses, but you don't strike me as the roses type. It's too expected, too easy. Every man in the florist shop ordered roses, including my dad. So I went with something unexpected, because that is exactly how I feel about you."

"Unexpected?" She wrinkled her brow, stepped through the doorway and froze in place.

The most delicious aroma emanated from her kitchen, where a covered pot simmered on the stove and a teapot steamed nearby on the counter. An embroidered linen cloth covered the table, set with her best dishes. Owen must have shown Tucker where they were. Tall candles stood in beautiful cut-crystal holders, waiting to be lit. The morning's dishes, which had been sitting in the sink, were gone, washed and put away.

This was definitely unexpected. "Tucker, I don't know what to say."

"Then don't say a thing. I've got dinner covered. Owen, Puddles and I are going to hang outside together for a while. Tea is steeping, so put up your feet and relax for a few minutes." He cupped her chin in one calloused, working man's hand. "Happy Valentine's Day."

"I can't be your valentine, Tucker. This isn't real. We both know it." Not that she didn't want it to be something that could last, but she had to keep her defenses up. She could not tumble any further for this man. She had more than Owen's heart to protect.

"For today, it's real. Today is all I'm asking for. It's all anyone has." He brushed a kiss to her forehead, the lightest of touches before granting her a dazzling grin, dimples and all, and loped out the door.

I will not fall in love with him, she vowed

as she unzipped her coat and slipped it over a hanger in the tiny entry closet. There were a hundred reasons why she had to be strong. She had to stop those unbidden wishes from turning into dreams of a happily-ever-after with Tucker.

Owen's laughter, muffled by the insulated walls, drew her to the window. Her son tossed a snowball at Tucker, who inched a bit into the path of the flying icy ball and took a hit directly in the chest. Tucker's baritone rumbled with humor and Owen punched the air, rejoicing in his hit. Puddles jumped and dashed, full of youthful energy.

Her defenses shattered. Every rationale silenced. Watching her son dodge a snowball obviously poorly aimed by Tucker and seeing the happiness on her child's dear face was the last blow. The man had done so much for the boy and, by extension, so much for her.

I'm in love with Tucker. She could no longer deny it. Worse, she feared Owen was in love with him, too.

Chapter Twelve

"One more chapter, Tucker. Please?"

It sure was tough to say no to the little guy. Tucker turned the page, the book a pleasant weight in his hand. Not that he would mind, but a glance at the bedside clock told him it was well after nine. Sitting at the foot of the bed, he shifted his weight, considering.

"No way." Sierra breezed through the doorway, never lovelier in his view than she was now in her pink sweatshirt and worn jeans. The look of censure in her gaze was only for show as she plucked the book out of his hands. "It's already past your bedtime as it is, Owen. The story can continue tomorrow."

"But Tucker won't be here tomorrow." Owen's eyes widened in a silent plea. He looked like he was putting all the might of his soul into that request. Those big, Bambi eyes sure would have moved him, Tucker reckoned.

"Yes, but you have school tomorrow." Sierra closed the book and laid it on the nightstand next to the plastic replica of Jack. "It's been a big day and it's time for Tucker to go home. Look how you've tired him out."

"Me, tired? I have only yawned a time or two," Tucker argued in his defense, enjoying the way Sierra turned her attention to him with the love for her son still glowing. She had a lot of responsibilities to shoulder alone. He liked knowing he'd lifted that burden for her, at least for tonight. He pushed off the twin bed. Puddles, at the foot of the mattress, stirred in his sleep. "Owen, I guess we have to do with your mom says."

"But you don't gotta finish the story." True concern dug into the boy's forehead. "I can tell you what happens."

"Sounds good, buddy." He jammed his hands into his pockets, wanting to ruffle the kid's hair or give him some other gesture of affection, but Sierra bent over him tucking the sheets tight. He took a step toward the door. "I'd like that."

"When?" Owen went up on one elbow.

"We'll let your mom decide. She's in charge." He paused at the doorway, on the periphery of the domestic scene as mother kissed her child on the forehead, tucked Slayer beside Owen and wished him sweet dreams. A soul-deep need to be in the middle of that circle overtook him, a longing too huge to measure. It was endless. Infinite. Never had he wanted anything as much.

"Good night," Owen murmured, sleep already claiming him as Tucker ambled down the hallway. He left Sierra to close the door softly and follow him.

The evening was at an end, the dishes were done. There was nothing left to do but leave. He knew Sierra started work early in the morning, but his boots dragged so he didn't head straight to the door. The evening had been fun—dinner conversation over spaghetti and garlic bread, Owen helping him with the dishes while they both did their best to charm Sierra, and the three of them on the couch watching a kid's movie. A mighty fine time. He wouldn't mind having more evenings just like this.

She emerged from the shadowed hallway, moving into the warm lamplight. He forgot to breathe. Oh, she was beautiful.

"So, the verdict?" He wanted to keep things light. She might shove him out the door if she knew what he was thinking. She saw a man who couldn't settle down—not a man who'd never had a reason to before. He'd never known how to open himself up enough.

He'd woken up in the ICU knowing he had a second chance to make things right. He'd learned that you never knew where life was about to take you—for good or bad. If God presented an opportunity for a blessing, then a smart man did not turn it down.

He had no doubt he was staring at a great blessing as Sierra eased onto the couch, luminous with a quiet beauty that captured him more with every look.

"The verdict for what?" She arched her brows, as if she had no clue what he was talking about.

"My kitchen skills." He moseyed over to the couch and sat next to her, not so close she would shy away and not so far he couldn't hold her hand if he got the chance. "Admit it. My spaghetti was superlative."

"Barely passable." A corner of her mouth hooked upward and her gray eyes, the same color as winter storm clouds, hinted that there was more to the story.

Call him curious. He wanted to know more. "Barely? It was a great deal more than that. One of the best recipes in the state."

"Oh, the state? An outrageous claim. There's no way to verify it."

"Then tell me this." He leaned in. "Did you like the meal I cooked for you?"

"More than you can imagine." She flipped her hair over her shoulder and relaxed into the corner of the couch.

"I can imagine a lot."

"In our seven years of marriage, Ricky didn't make one meal." The humor fell away, leaving only the sadness of memories she didn't like to unearth. "Not once did he carry a single plate from the table to the sink. It didn't matter if I was sick, if I was pregnant or if I was exhausted from being up all night with a colicky baby. So, yes, I liked it very much."

"Good. That was the idea." Tucker's good humor dazzled, but it was his seriousness that could steal every last piece of her admiration. He had sincerity that radiated through every part of him.

What was she going to do about her growing love for him? Somehow she had to stop it. She set her chin, determined to find some way to put a much-needed barrier between them. But could she?

No. Her neurons refused to think of a single plan to drive him away.

"I'm not afraid of hard work. Housework, barn work or something else." He didn't blink, he didn't balk as his hand covered hers with the strength and heat of a brand. Never had he appeared so strong. He could be a western legend, a hero in a story too good to be true. "I see something that needs doing, and I do it. It's the way I was raised. It's who I am."

"Why are you telling me this?" Worse, why was her pulse flatlining? Why did it feel as if she were falling into a whirlpool, spinning around and down without escape.

"Because I want you to see that in me." His jaw hardened into granite, resolute. "I want to come courting."

"Courting?" Her throat spasmed, closing shut momentarily, making it impossible to breathe or speak.

"You know, when a man is serious about a woman, they go out on dates." Dimples etched into his stone features, softening the rough edges. "He brings her flowers. You've heard of this social custom before?"

Somehow her stunned neurons managed to work together well enough. She bobbed her head in a semblance of a nod.

"Good. Because I like spending time with you." The layers of his voice vibrated with feeling she could not help but respond to. He leaned in near enough to brush the tip of his nose with hers. So fathomless, those eyes, and as blue as dreams. His mouth slanted over hers. "I want to spend more time together. Okay?"

Yes. The single word rose up like a solemn prayer, full of need and respect. If her mind was working properly, she would have been able to hold back that foolish yes, to tamp it down and let reason prevail. His lips brushed hers softly like the lightest notes in a song. His kiss was over too soon to savor as he searched her eyes for his answer.

An answer that could be yes.

When she wanted nothing more than to ask him to stay for a bit longer, she pushed to her feet. She could not allow herself to wonder what it would be like to lay her cheek against the marble expanse of his chest. She could not wonder how safe it might feel to be sweetly enfolded in his arms.

"The thing is…" she began, searching for the right words. She didn't want to hurt him. "I have Owen to consider."

"Sure, I know that." The room seemed to shrink as Tucker rose from the couch. All six feet three inches of vital, larger-than-life man overshadowed her. As if he were vulnerable and his heart on the line, he winced. "Owen and I get along pretty good, don't you think?"

"Very much. Maybe too good."

"That's a bad thing?"

No, she wanted to say. Tenderness welled up, making it hard to find her voice. Even if she wanted to discover where a relationship with Tucker would take her, she didn't have that luxury. Panic ripped through her veins, a fear she could safely ignore because Owen was her primary concern, her first responsibility. "You have made my son so happy, but he's getting attached."

"He's not the only one. I care for him, too." A muscle worked in his jaw. "You are a package deal. I care for you both."

"That's not a good idea." That was the understatement of the century. She fisted her hands to keep from reaching out and soothing the crinkles digging into brackets around his sad mouth. She did not want to hurt him, although it was too late. She took a shaky breath. "Owen is going to miss you when you go back to rodeo life."

"And I'll miss him. Maybe you've heard of the telephone? I could use it to call and talk to him. I might even use it to talk to you." Humor enriched the deep notes of his voice, but it could not hide the pain. "I'm not cutting off all ties just because I'm going back to work. I can fly in for visits. Exchange email. Use chat rooms. Send text messages."

It was the silent plea in his compelling blue irises that touched her most. She loved this side of Tucker, a part of him that had been there all along, buried beneath the easygoing charm. But was he a man she could count on? She did not have the strength to find out. Seven long years of a disappointing marriage had taken their toll on her, and Owen had been hurt too much.

She took a breath, struggling for the right words. "I'm certain you will continue to be kind to my son, but it can't be anything more than friendship. Don't you see? I can't open him up to that kind of uncertainty. He needs his world to be secure, especially after the way his father treated him."

"Sure, I understand." Agony flashed in his eyes. In the next blink, it was gone. "I've always intended to buy up some land around here, preferably something near the family ranch, and raise a herd, maybe even sheep."

"One day, you should." She bowed her head, slipping away into the shadows near the kitchen. A closet door opened and when he looked next, she held his coat in her hand. "I'm going to miss you, Tucker."

"This is good-bye? We can't even be friends?"

"Why? There would be no point. I would always look at you and want—" She fell silent, her blond hair curtaining her face, shielding her emotions. When she finished her sentence, her voice had strengthened, full of resolve, all traces of vulnerability gone. "Let's just say I'm busy. Owen is my life. Providing for him, caring for him, being a mother to him, it's all I have time for."

"Sure. I get that." He was crushed. Saying anything different would be a lie. He took the coat from her and headed for the door. No night had ever seemed as dark or a winter's snow as bleak. He headed into the storm, leaving Sierra and his heart behind.

She stood at the window, the drape in hand, watching the pickup's taillights disappear in the dark. Tucker was gone, and she'd hurt him. After every kind thing he'd done for her and Owen. Her stomach bunched up tight and she wrapped her arms around her middle to contain the knot of sorrow. The curtain fell back into place. Reminders of Tucker were everywhere. The flowers scented the air as the heater clicked on, the scent of tomato, basil and garlic lingered in the kitchen, the chair at the table he'd sat in, empty now.

I did the right thing, Lord. She had to find comfort in that, although solace was hard to find. It eluded her as she sat on the couch where Tucker had been. It evaded her as she turned on the TV to the movie in the DVD player Owen had picked out and the three of them had watched together. It was one of the movies Tucker had brought Owen during his hospital stay.

The phone shattered the silence. She snatched it up, her pulse fast and erratic. A part of her hoped Tucker would be on the line. "Hello?"

"Hi, dear." Jeri Lynn sounded more chipper than ever. "I had to call and check how your evening went. The wait is killing me."

"Oh, Mom." She sank onto the cushion and covered her forehead with her free hand. The rush of emotions overwhelmed her. Love was terrible. The horrible downs, the inconsistent ups, the roller coaster ride that had left her abandoned and devastated. Why had she ever let her affections build for Tucker? "It wasn't my evening, not really. Tucker cooked for Owen, played in the snow with him and watched a movie with him."

"With you, too." Jeri Lynn was smart enough to read between the lines.

Sierra sighed, hating to admit the truth. "Yes, with me, too."

"It's a serious man who cooks a meal for a woman, especially on Valentine's Day." Mom sounded as if she were having a grand time. It was easy to picture her in her favorite chair by the fireplace, the hearth roaring and crackling, with Dad watching a sports show in the opposite chair. "I had just pulled into your driveway after picking up Owen from day care. I couldn't believe my eyes when this black pickup rambled up behind me. Owen shouting, 'It's Tucker! It's Tucker!' gave me a clue who it was."

So easy to picture. She tried to pretend she didn't care. "It's been a real thrill for him to befriend his rodeo hero."

"Oh, it seems like a good deal more than befriending. I have eyes. I saw the look on that young man's face. He's smitten."

"Tucker's returning to the rodeo circuit once his doctor clears it. End of discussion. Mom, how was Cady's open house?"

"I'll let you change the subject because I love you and you're my favorite daughter."

"I'm your only daughter." There were hundreds of reasons not to be pining after Tucker, not to be upset at how she'd ended things with him. She had Owen. She had a wonderful mom and dad, she had friends and extended family she wouldn't trade for anything. She had a comfortable home she'd bought a year ago on three acres of land. She had more reasons than that, but none came to mind. This house had never felt lonely like this, empty, as if something vitally important was gone.

"I'll let you change the subject, but I reserve the right to come back to it. Cady's open house was a raving success. What a beautiful inn. She is such a sweetheart. Hard to believe she was a tough, successful big-city lawyer." Mom paused. "I heard something about the diner having problems. That's just a rumor, isn't it?"

"I'm afraid not." They talked for a few more minutes about the owner's situation, Sierra doing her best to skirt the issue of reduced wages and income, and bid her mother good-night. The heavy, suffocating silence returned after she hung up the phone.

She wasn't too happy with herself. She wanted to forget the look of hurt on Tucker's face, but she couldn't. She was too afraid to open her heart and she'd never told him.

She hadn't let him know it was her fault—not his. She hit the remote, the TV screen blinked off and she hung her head. The wind picked up, driving cold into the room and into the chambers of her soul.

It was a hard ride home. Behind the wheel Tucker turned up the CD player so the cheerful twang of country music could drown out the fact that he was alone. He slowed down at the edge of town, although he doubted Ford, the town's only lawman, would be set up with his radar in the library parking lot. Ford had better things to do, such as giving Autumn a memorable Valentine's Day, as a good prospective husband should. Tucker didn't doubt Ford was up to the challenge.

Town was dark and quiet, the streetlights glowing in the white of the storm, and his were the only tire tracks on the main street. As the wipers swished and flakes flew at the glass in a ghostly dance, he did his best to keep his mind on the road. It didn't stay there. He sped up on the edge of town, leaving the light behind. Country darkness closed in around him.

She may have rejected him romantically, but he'd caught the look on her face. Hesitation and sadness permeated her with a force she couldn't hide. He felt the aftereffects of it like a shadow in the night. She had her reasons why she couldn't see him again all laid out and prepared—rational, sensible and selfless. Owen was the reason. Owen needed stability and security. Owen's heart needed protecting.

Perhaps not just Owen's heart. Maybe Sierra's, too. His grip tightened on the wheel as he steered through the storm. She hadn't been able to disguise one poignant look of longing, as if for the sweetest of wishes, and he couldn't get that picture out of his head. Her honest beauty, her loving spirit, her gentle soul made everything in his world small by comparison.

The rodeo—that had never been anything but passing time, a way to escape the emotional ties that always made him uncomfortable. Emotional ties still made him uneasy, but he was learning to open his heart. He wanted to be for her what his dad had been for him. Solid and dependable, like a fixed mark that would not move, change or break. He wanted to give her so many things, to take care of her, to solve her every problem and to stand between her and any hardship.

If only she would let him.

He slowed at a crossroads since visibility was poor. No one was coming so he continued on. Sierra had grown up at the far end of that road, where her parents still lived. As the wind gusted against the side of the truck, he remembered that petite, shy little girl with the golden braids and a book always in hand.

She had grown up, matured and learned how to put him in his place—he would never dare tug on her braids now—but she was not so different. Her home was full of books filed on shelves, books stacked on tables, even piled by Owen's bed. Tucker pushed his sadness aside. He was still that same school-age boy with a heart that had never loved another.

Only her.

It may have taken him nearly twenty years to figure it out, but he finally got it.

The truck carried him past Mr. Green's driveway, the headlights illuminating briefly a For Sale sign tacked to a fence post. He wondered how Cotton was faring, now that he was safely home. Owen sure had a grand time riding him. Maybe he would have to drop by and visit the sheep and talk with Mr. Green. Maybe Sierra simply needed proof of his intentions. She had to know he was a man who stuck to his course once he made a commitment.

The lights of home shone through the storm as he drove up the hill, and a glowing sense of peace filled him. *Home.* No word had ever sounded as good. He pulled into the garage, already looking forward to seeing his dad. Maybe they'd share a root beer in front of the television, watch a sports show, an old movie or the news. It sounded good. Time rolled by, ticking away like a bomb, and he didn't want to miss any more time with his dad and those he loved.

He shook the flakes off his coat and stomped the snow off his boots at the back door. The moment he stepped inside, warmth hit him, both physical and emotional. He recalled being a little boy stomping into the mudroom, kicking off his boots in a hurry to get a freshly baked cookie from Aunt Opal. He remembered being a teenager, tossing schoolbooks onto the table in a hurry to take Jack out for a run. So many good times—his sisters' chatter, Dad's laughter, Justin's banter, the holidays and celebrations and losses that had drawn them all closer together.

"Hi there, son." Frank looked up from the table, a telephone book open to the yellow pages in front of him, the cordless phone in one hand. "Were you out with Sierra and Owen?"

"We stayed in, actually. I cooked them

dinner." He ambled across the floor in his stocking feet and headed for the fridge.

"A working mom ought to like that quite a bit." Frank smiled. The phone book closed with a snap. "Did she like her flowers?"

"She didn't toss me out on my ear for sending them to her." Humor came easier. He wasn't ready to talk about his plans just yet. Besides, he still had a few things to figure out. He took two cans from the refrigerator shelf and closed the door. "Any word from Cady?"

"She liked her roses." Dad pushed back his chair and stood. "I made a reservation at the steak house in Sunshine we like so well."

"So, she said yes. A shocker. I don't know what she was thinking."

"A lapse in her good judgment, no doubt." With a chuckle, Frank sank the phone into its holder. "Now I have to actually take her out. I'm twisted up in knots over this date. I don't know how you kids do it."

"You get numb to the agony of dating

after a while." His dad could joke, and so could he. He understood what his father was sidestepping. The risk that went along with wanting to give a woman your heart was a perilous one. One he was still smarting from. He held out a can. "We can forget our troubles watching TV."

"Good plan, son." Dad popped the top on his root beer. "Your cousin called a few minutes ago."

"Sean? Is he coming out to lend a hand?" Tucker led the way into the living room.

"Yep. He flies in on Friday. I thought you could swing by the airport and pick him up."

"Sure. I'll be in Sunshine anyway for my doctor's appointment." The day of truth. Would he be able to return to riding, or would it be another two weeks of physical therapy staying right here, where he could work on changing Sierra's mind?

Autumn looked up from the couch, a bridal magazine on her lap and a stack piled on the coffee table in front of her. "Hey. How did things go with Sierra?"

"Hard to say. She's still talking to me, so that's a good sign." She hadn't closed the door completely on their relationship. He would never forget the pure caring in her gaze as she'd rejected him. He loved her. It was as simple as that. He thought there might be a chance she loved him, too. "How about you and Ford?"

"Fantastic. He took me to Cady's inn for dinner. Everyone must have had the same idea, because the place was packed. Folks were waiting in the lobby for almost two hours." She glanced at a wedding dress on a glossy page, shrugged and closed the magazine. "We saw Rori and Justin in the dining room. They are spending the night there. I hear the rooms are luxuriously comfortable and country gorgeous. Rori couldn't stop raving. I couldn't believe how good the food was. Cady must have brought in a renowned chef from somewhere. Take Sierra there for your next date. She will adore it."

"I'll keep that in mind." He dropped into one of the chairs.

"Great. Thanks for mentioning that." Dad looked unusually pale as he sank into the sectional. "If that's the kind of food she's used to, I need to cancel my reservation."

"Don't," Autumn advised. "I know Cady well enough. She might be city raised, but she's a country girl at heart."

"I hope you're right." Dad didn't sound so sure about it.

Poor Dad. Tucker knew just how he felt. The phone sang out an electronic tune and he hopped to his feet. Could be a chance Sierra had mulled things over and wanted to change the answer she'd given him. "I'll get it."

It was Cheyenne's number on the caller ID. He swallowed back disappointment and plucked up the cordless. "Howdy."

"Tucker? Is Autumn there?" Cheyenne sounded strained, as if on the verge of tears. A sniffle confirmed it.

"Sure. What's wrong?" He would stop the world from turning if it would protect his sisters.

"Can I please talk to her?" A sob tore her words apart.

His heart, too. His younger sister was hurting. Before he could call out, Autumn sauntered into the kitchen.

"What's wrong?" Concern knit her face.

He held the receiver out to her. "Cheyenne is crying. That can't be good on Valentine's Day."

"No, it can't." Sadly, she took the phone, her voice dropping as she walked in the direction of the family room. "What happened, Cheye?"

Heartbreak. That was the result when love didn't work out, when romance didn't turn into a happily-ever-after. Not ready to give up on Sierra, Tucker retraced his steps. Dad had clicked on the television and a sitcom released canned laughter into the room.

"Is Cheyenne okay?" Dad asked.

"I don't know." Tucker dropped into his chair, wondering about Sierra. Was she missing him, too?

Chapter Thirteen

"So, how is your romance going along?" Happy anticipation wreathed Mrs. Tipple's lovely face. The elderly lady plopped a sugar cube into her tea. "I heard Tucker had flowers delivered for Valentine's Day."

"No comment." Sierra slipped the generous slice of blueberry cheesecake into the center of the table. The door opened, letting in a rush of cool air and damp. Rain fell steadily, washing away the last of the snow on the ground. Fitting, she decided, since she wanted to forget Valentine's Day. Tightness bunched in her throat as she slid four dessert plates onto the table along with four spoons. "Do you ladies need anything else?"

"Just an answer, young lady." Mrs. Tipple twinkled. She was trouble through and through—the best kind of trouble.

"Yes, we're dying to know," Mrs. Plum chimed in. "It's been a while since any of us have been young and in love."

"Speak for yourself, Vera." Mrs. Parnell chuckled. "I'm still in love with my husband."

"Oh, yes. I forgot. Me, too." Mrs. Plum dissolved into laughter. "Forgive me. I meant dating. Being courted by a man is so, so sweet."

"Not nearly as sweet as a lifetime spent happily as his wife," Mrs. Parnell pointed out.

Too sweet. Sierra adored these elderly women. "I'm going to cut off the tea. You ladies have had way too much."

"Good idea, dear," Mrs. Tipple agreed.

With a smile, Sierra padded away, leaving behind her a rise of merry giggles. The door whooshed open and she skidded to a halt in the middle of the aisle.

Tucker. He'd never looked so formidable. He filled the doorway with his remarkable shoulders and impressive physique. Dark hair windswept, blue eyes striking, expression determined, he radiated authority and confidence and masculinity. He was every wish she could not want and every dream she could not pray for.

"Do you have a minute?" The notes of his familiar baritone struck like a hammer. Tension corded his neck and bunched along his muscled jaw.

"Of course. Grab a table." She gestured to the row of empty booths. The lunch crowd wasn't exactly bustling these days. Her tables were fine for now, their orders taken and meals delivered.

Why was he here? She walked after him, the rubber soles of her shoes squeaking slightly with her gait. Why would he interrupt her in the middle of the day? There was only one reason she could think of. Her toe stubbed the floor, pitching her forward. Off balance, she righted herself, blushing, hoping no one had noticed, especially Tucker. He'd come to tell her good-bye. That's why he was here. Her knees trembled as she slid onto a booth cushion.

"You look good." Not a trace of humor highlighted his face. She had never seen him this serious, not even on the morning of Tucker's surgery.

"Thanks. You, too." It was a good thing she'd stood firm. She didn't doubt he cared for her and she knew he cared a great deal for Owen, but that would not stop him from leaving. With his next breath he would tell her he was heading out for Dallas or Tulsa or wherever. It's been nice knowing you, he'd say and she couldn't appear crushed. She'd turned him down. She couldn't let him know what he meant to her.

"The doctor gave me a clean bill of health." The tension didn't slip off his stoney features. A note of hardness rang in his voice. "I'm cleared to ride again. I've got a little more strengthening I need to do before I can compete, but I'm almost there. I'm fully recovered."

"Congratulations." She held her chin high, truly glad for him. "Riding makes you happy."

"A lot of things do." He reached into his coat pocket and pulled out a thick fold of papers. He smoothed the creases out of them with deliberate care. "Spending time at home has been good for me. I always dash in and race back to the airport, too busy to sink into life here. This injury forced me do it. I think I was always in a hurry because I was afraid if I wasn't, it would be too tough to leave."

"You are close to your family, especially your dad." She understood that. She felt the same way about hers. If love for his family wasn't enough to hold him here, then his simple affection for her wouldn't be nearly enough. She had to accept it, regardless of how much it hurt. "Of course it will be hard to leave them."

"It will be hard to leave." He spread the papers on the table. "Look what I have."

"Is it a legal document?" A furrow dug into her forehead.

"A purchase and sale agreement." He turned the pages around for her to easily read them. "The Greens are retiring and I'm buying their ranch, livestock and all."

"Even Cotton?"

"He's my number one animal. I plan to take extra special care of him." It was only the start of his plans, but the rest was up to her. He straightened his spine, ignored the jackhammer force of his pulse and hoped his vulnerabilities were well hidden. "I'll keep him for Owen to ride anytime."

"That's nice of you, Tucker." Her peaceful smile held no trace of sorrow that he was leaving and not a hint that she might accept him if he were to ask. She glanced at the agreement and nudged it toward him. "Frank must be ecstatic. Is your family going to look after the land and livestock for you?"

"I imagine they will lend a hand when it's needed." He took a deep breath, knowing he had to play this cool, keep defenses up around his heart just enough so that when she rejected him, the pain wouldn't show. It was a risk to ask her like this, but he wanted to do it where Owen wouldn't overhear. He braced himself for the worst and forged ahead. "Whether I leave town or not depends on you."

"On me?" She tilted her head to one side. Her bangs swept her puzzled forehead. She couldn't have looked more confused. "I don't understand."

Okay, that is not a good sign. He figured she might have put the pieces together by now. He lowered his voice so the entire diner wouldn't hear. "You said Owen needs security. Well, this is as secure as it gets. I'm putting down roots and I'm prepared to keep any promise you let me make."

Her jaw slid open. Her pretty rosebud mouth shaped into an O. She didn't move. Maybe she wasn't prepared for him to make any promises. That cut deep, but he didn't let it show. He hoped he'd hidden the wince of pain well enough from her view. She had no idea what she meant to him. Not a clue. Maybe he should tell her.

"I'm ready to settle down. I've signed on the dotted line and forked over no small amount of earnest money. The sale is final at the end of the month." He had to say the words that frightened him most, but he was tough and not even something as serious and potentially dangerous as committed love could scare him. Just please don't hurt me, he begged silently. "I love you, Sierra. I want to court you, marry you, grow old with you. Do you feel the same?"

Her gray eyes darkened like a sky before a storm, so poignant with silent sadness. He saw her answer in the hitch of her breath and the bow of her head. She traced the edge of the Formica tabletop with her forefinger, thinking it over—not his offer, but how to reject him.

"Sierra!" Nate Cannon, the local veterinarian, held up his cup, unaware of what was going on. "Can I get a refill to go?"

"Sure thing." Stilted, she stumbled out of the booth. True apology was spelled on her face. "Tucker, I'll be right back."

"Fine." He didn't mind waiting. The reprieve would give him time to prepare for the final blow. Being rejected by Sierra wasn't nearly as painful as being in love with her. She sailed down the aisle, unaware what she was doing to him. He folded up the agreement and shoved it back into his pocket. His phone rang, so he answered it.

"Are you going to be much longer?" Sean asked, anxious to get settled in at the ranch. "I don't mind waiting in the truck, but I'm starting to get hungry."

"I need another minute," he told his cousin and hung up. He would need more than a minute to recover—*if* recovering from losing Sierra was even possible.

She moved like music with a soft lilt and cadence of her own as she poured a cup for Nate, grabbed two plates from the kitchen and sashayed down the aisle. She handed out the meals, gave Nate his coffee and finally paced back to Tucker reluctantly. Everything in him stilled as she slipped into the booth.

"I need more stability for Owen than you can give, Tucker." Gently spoken, with a request for forgiveness soft in her voice.

Her rejection hit him hard. Nothing could soften it. Air whooshed out of his lungs. Pain cracked through him like bones breaking. He'd known her answer would be no. Whatever hopes had driven him in here plummeted to the floor and shattered. Left with the pieces, he wasn't sure what to do now. "What more do you want?"

"You've been in our lives less than two months. You waltz in and right now you're ready to waltz out. Who is to say your feelings won't be the same?" She pitched her voice low, as the diner silenced. Perhaps she was aware of several patrons leaning in their direction, appearing not to be listening, although they were. She paused to glance around. Then, as if there was nothing else to be done, she finished it. "You could charm your way into a romance with me and right back out again. Relationships come with no guarantee, but I have to be cautious. Owen has had a lot of promises broken."

"And so have you."

She nodded, tears shining in her eyes. That was the part he didn't know how to fix. How to make her see his love for her. She was a country girl, not someone who would want grand gestures or elaborate protestations. It wasn't easy, but he had to tell her the truth. "I'm not waltzing into anything. I've loved you forever. I always will."

She swallowed hard, considering his words. "Love isn't always enough."

"Mine is." He leaned in closer, his gaze intense, his voice layered with affection. "The real question is this. Do you love me?"

"Not enough." Not enough to let go of her fears. Not enough to believe. Looking into his gaze and seeing him made her want to. She fisted her hands, fought the rat-tat-tat of panic in her chest. She thought of all the ways he could let her down without meaning to, like Ricky, who'd made promises he'd intended to keep and couldn't. Tucker had good intentions.

She had no trust left. All she could see was reaching out, needing him to help, to be there for her, to be there for Owen and hearing the door close as he walked away. It was Ricky's voice she heard as he'd packed his things. "I've had enough. Enough problems, enough demands, enough bills. All I do is work and work some more. This isn't fun."

"What about Owen?" she'd asked.

"I'll call him when I get to Reno." The suitcase had slammed shut and he'd hauled it off the bed, facing her, packed and ready to go.

"What about me?" The question had felt torn out of her.

"I don't care anymore." His affection had turned to contempt and she didn't know why as he'd shouldered past her and out the door.

Leaving her alone with a sobbing little boy, her own heartbreak. She would find out later about the unpaid rent, overdue bills and less than a hundred dollars in the bank account.

Not all marriages went down that path, she knew, but how could she trust Tucker? She wanted to. He was sincere, loyal and his heart was big enough, but he had recognition, fame within the rodeo set, a lifestyle that took him away for a part of the year and no history of staying put. What if she needed him, truly leaned on him, and he let her down? What if one day the going got tough and he took one look at her and Owen and decided they weren't worth the work and dedication love took?

Her heart was scarred enough. "You weren't here, so you don't know how devastating it was when Ricky walked out on me. I had a little boy broken, who cried himself to sleep every night for an entire year missing his daddy. I was left holding the pieces of a shattered life I didn't know if I could put back together. About the time I managed to find an even keel, Owen was diagnosed with his heart condition and we were plunged into chaos again."

"But I was there for you both at the hospital, wasn't I?" His hand covered hers, warm as a kept promise, solid as a committed vow.

"Yes, but I can't risk it. For Owen's sake."

"And yours." The man saw everything, his tone so low, she could hardly hear his words. His gaze intensified, holding her captive as if he saw clearly her weakness.

"I can't give my heart again. It's just better this way." She might love him, but no promises had been made. This was the best time to walk away. "We can be friends."

"I don't want to be friends." He withdrew, sorrow etching its way across his features and into her heart.

She didn't want him to go. She wanted to keep him from leaving, to confess her feelings, to grab at this chance for happiness.

But that's all it was—a chance. She'd made that leap of faith and failed once. All she could see was how very much it would hurt Owen if a relationship didn't work out with Tucker.

And how very much it would hurt her.

"Sierra!" Sandi called from the back, unaware of the conversation taking place. "Order up!"

"I'd better go." He braced both hands on the tabletop, leveling his substantial frame out of the booth. Rising above her, he seemed to go on forever, so large and impressive in her view that no other man could compare.

If only she wasn't so afraid, she would tell him the truth. That she was clinging to denial with all her might. She had done more than fall in love with him. She'd gone so far there was no turning back. He had a hold on her heart forever.

Just tell him, Sierra. She took a deep breath, rising from the bench seat and searching for the words. There were none.

What she found instead were the images of packed suitcases, the echoed knell of boots walking down the hall and the front door squeaking open.

The fear that he didn't love her enough wrapped around her like a straitjacket, keeping her from confessing the truth. She loved him too much to be hurt like that again.

"Good-bye, Tucker." It took all her willpower to keep her voice from cracking. "Will you be leaving soon?"

"Immediately." He hurt, too. The evidence shone in his shadowed eyes, pinched in the corners of his mouth, radiated from him like ice on a wintry wind. "Take care, Sierra. Tell Owen I'll call him from the road tomorrow."

"He'll like that." Her throat closed. This was her last chance to tell him not to go, but she feared he would leave anyway. Hadn't he said there was email, text messaging, internet chat rooms. Lots of ways to keep in touch with Owen. With Owen.

Not with her. Unable to speak, she lifted

her hand and managed to waggle a few fingers in a semblance of a wave.

"Good-bye, Sierra." His voice caught,
a silent plea crossed his handsome face.
When she didn't respond, his wide shoulders
slumped. As if gathering up his strength,
his spine straightened, the pain disappeared
from his chiseled features. He walked
through the door and out of her life.

Cady Winslow studied her reflection in
the cheval mirror, not recognizing herself. A
strange woman stared back at her, one with
a secret sparkling in her green eyes and her
cheeks flushed with excitement. She was
going on a date with Frank Granger. She
still couldn't believe it.

She'd heard his story from several women
friends at his oldest son's wedding a while
ago in December. After Frank's wife ran
out on him and left him with five kids to
raise, he had taken Lainie back when she'd
fallen ill and she'd needed someone to care
for her. The mayor's wife said Lainie had

ruined Frank for all women. He'd never looked at another woman in all those long years since.

Until her.

Don't get your hopes up too high. That was a sure path to disappointment. She straightened her silk jacket and debated changing her shoes again, but footsteps charging down the narrow hall in her direction made her forget about her shoes entirely.

"Aunt Cady! Aunt Cady!" Her goddaughters tumbled into her bedroom in a flurry of little-girl excitement, not that they were *that* little these days. Jenny was twelve going on thirty, and Julianna a sweet, innocent ten.

"Girls, what do you think?" She loved these children as if they were her flesh and blood. They were honorary family, since she'd babysat their father, Adam, years ago when she was a teenager. She squinted at her earrings. Perhaps the pearls were too sedate.

"You're pretty." Julianna spoke first and

grabbed hold of Cady's hand. "But we need to talk about the horses."

"You mean my horse?" She brushed a way-ward lock of brown hair that had escaped her ponytail out of the girl's face. While she loved that they had come out to help celebrate the opening of her inn, she loathed that they had to leave. "I promise I will let you ride Misty again first thing tomorrow before you all leave for the airport."

"I know. I mean the other horses." Juli-anna gave a tug. "The ones you are *going* to get."

"Oh, for my stables." Cady laughed, always charmed by the ardent animal lover. "Do you have some advice for me?"

"I've been thinking about it." The girl's brow furrowed with concentration. "You should get nice horses."

"I'll put nice on the list." She thanked Jenny, who handed her a pearl necklace to wear. Cady gathered her hair in a makeshift ponytail and knelt to let the older girl secure the clasp. "What else?"

"You should get them from the shelter." Julianna dropped onto the foot of the bed with a bounce. "Because it's important to save animals."

What a dear heart. Cady couldn't say no to that. "I promise I will save every horse I buy. I'll have my manager get right on it. Okay?"

"Okay." Julianna's smile could light up the world.

The doorbell rang, jolting terror straight into Cady's bloodstream. Frank was here! Her blood pressure shot into the red zone. Boy, was she nervous. At one last glance in the mirror, she shrugged. It was the best she could do. Time had run out to fuss and second-guess her wardrobe choices.

"C'mon, Aunt Cady." Jenny touched her sleeve. "You look nice. Like a magazine cover."

"Not true, but I love you for saying so." She hugged both girls. Male voices murmured from the front of the cottage. Adam and Frank exchanging greetings, from the sound of it. She didn't want to keep him waiting, so she grabbed her little evening purse and marched the girls ahead of her down the short hallway and into the warmth of the living room, where two men stood in the entry. Only one man stole every ounce of her attention and the entire focus of her gaze. Frank looked incomparable in a dark dinner jacket, tie and slacks. His snowy shirt contrasted pleasantly with his sun-browned complexion.

Be still my heart, she thought. Never had a man affected her so much. Never had she been a basket of nerves. He was her most secret prayer come to life. She so wanted the evening to go well and the fear it might be a disaster tortured her. Taking on her first cross-examination in front of a judge and jury hadn't been as terrifying.

"Cady." Frank's richly layered baritone warmed immeasurably as he said her name. His mile-wide shoulders straightened, his chest lifted and the appreciation respectfully shining in his blue gaze was the best gift he could have given her. The flowers he handed her couldn't compare. "I was just talking to Adam about little Owen Baker. He saved that boy's life. We're all grateful."

"Just doing my job," Adam added gruffly, not at all aware of the difference he had made. It was a difference he made every day. Because he cared so much, she could tell the long hours and dedication were taking their toll, along with the aftermath of a painful divorce. She worried he might burn out, a shame for a caring doctor. Adam raked a hand through his brown hair, obviously uncomfortable. "You two have fun."

"We'll try." She handed the flowers to Jenny, who was closest, and kissed each girl on the cheek. Then she slipped into the coat Frank insisted on holding for her and walked through the door he insisted on opening for her.

Her hopes were definitely way too high as she stepped across her cottage's tiny porch and into the rain. Frank was ready with an umbrella, bless him, and held it overhead as he escorted her to his truck.

"This is a Wyoming Cadillac," he quipped as he opened the door and gave her a hand up onto the leather seat. "It's not fancy."

Was he self-conscious, too? She laid her hand on the cuff of his jacket. The gesture surprised her and she knew when his eyes widened that it had surprised him, too. Really endearing. She relaxed a notch. "Do you know what Autumn says about me?"

"Knowing my daughter, it has to be something good. She likes you."

"And I like her. She says I'm a country girl down deep." Cady had discovered it was true. She missed the life she'd left behind in Manhattan, but even as a young girl she'd dreamed of wide-open skies and having a horse as one of her best friends. Of running a beautiful inn full of pretty rooms and friendly people.

She'd taken the long way to her dream, working her way up to senior partner, but early retirement had brought her not only here to her childhood dreams but to new ones she'd given up on. Romance had found her. But would it work out?

Lord, please. I've never wanted anything so much.

"That's good news," Frank quipped in his relaxed, sweet-humored manner. "Because I made reservations at a steak house. There's a French restaurant over in Sunshine, but I'd rather not go there. I'm not gonna eat snails."

"That's two of us." She laughed, she couldn't help it. Her nerves had disappeared. The rain poured down with hurricane force, but it felt like the sunniest of days because of the man who tugged out her seat belt and helped her click the buckle. He closed her door against the rain with a humble, gentlemanly strength that captured her heart ever more.

Chapter Fourteen

Nerves were still giving Frank a bit of trouble, but all in all he figured things were going great for a first date. He took a swallow of cola. "How's your steak?"

"Divine. Filet mignon is one of my favorites. I insisted it had to be on the inn's menu." The dim lighting did her justice—any lighting did. Her sleek hair shone with deep russets and polished chestnuts and honeyed browns framing her endearing, heart-shaped face. With her radiant skin and emerald-green eyes, she was the most beautiful woman he'd ever laid eyes on. Her movements were elegant as she sliced a dainty piece of beef. "My chef is someone I brought out from New York. She was a client of mine."

"It's hard to see you as a cutthroat attorney. Not that you aren't smart enough," he was quick to add.

"I love the law. It is incredibly fascinating, not that there aren't flaws. Nothing is perfect, but I set out to use my talents to help people." She set down her knife on the edge of her plate. In the play of muted light, her caring spirit shone through. "I think I accomplished that."

"You like making a difference." Easy to see. Easy to like. He set down his knife and stabbed a piece of beef, gathering up his courage to turn the conversation to the personal. "Why didn't you ever marry?"

"I had a fiancé once." Sadness flashed in her jewel-green irises. "Oh, I was young. We met in our first year at law school. He was a serious student, too. We studied together and then when we were done, we studied some more together. We were close for years."

"Did he break your heart? Or did you break his?"

"A little of both." At least she was honest. "Over time, we both began to see we were very different people. He wanted a stay-at-home wife. I wanted to ace my bar exam and start as a junior associate in a well-respected firm."

The sadness returned, and he hated that she had known disappointment of any kind. He wanted to fix that for her and to keep it from happening again. "I know something about finding yourself worlds apart from the person you love and not sure how you got there."

"That was exactly what happened. I thought we were heading in one direction, so by the time I realized I was standing alone on that path it was too late." She poked the tines of her fork into a sautéed half moon of zucchini squash on her plate. "He made me choose. So I took my bar exam."

"Any regrets?"

"Now and then. I didn't want to marry

a man who would make me choose like that."

"No, he didn't understand your heart."

"Exactly." Amazing how she and Frank got along so well. The evening had been perfect, the conversation as easy as breathing. It was unexpected and thrilling and right, all wrapped up in one. She studied the zucchini stuck on her fork. "I made the right choice. God has richly blessed my career, so I'm sure I followed His path, but there was never anyone else."

"I find that hard to believe." Frank watched her with a resplendent intensity she'd never experienced before. It made her want to all at once blush and hide and hold tight to this moment, to never let it end. He leaned in, listening intently. "There was no one since law school? That's a long stretch of lonely."

"Yes." He'd pegged it exactly. "I filled my time with work. Demanding work and so much of it, time sped by and I didn't notice it. I dated, but nothing turned serious. Things just didn't work out."

It was better to gloss over the emptiness she'd felt when she would stumble into her building late, the sounds of life from other apartments permeating the walls as she ambled down the hall to her door. Her key turning the bolt would echo and the place felt vacant as she closed the door behind her. No one to greet her. No laughter of family, no interesting conversations. She would turn on the television to cover up the silence. She may have moved away, but those things hadn't changed. She winced. "How about you?"

"Me?" He took another sip of cola, setting the glass down with careful deliberation, gathering his thoughts. "Time sped by for me, too. As if running a cattle ranch wasn't enough to keep me on my toes, I raised five kids mostly on my own. I had to think about their needs first."

"Of course. Your commitment to them shows, Frank. You have a wonderful family."

"Thanks. Those kids are my great

treasures." He shrugged a shoulder self-consciously. He didn't look like a man comfortable with feelings, but he forged ahead anyway. "After the youngest, Addy, was off to college I could have started dating but I wasn't ready. I suppose you heard that, too."

"Yes." She took a bite and watched him specula-tively.

"Truth is I never thought I would try again." He firmed his jaw and dug deep for the courage he needed. "When Lainie came back sick and dying and I had to take her in, it about killed me. I did it because of my kids. Lainie was their mother. I took care of her, made sure she had the finest medical and nursing care, and I put aside my broken heart. Every time I saw her, those pieces broke more. By the time she was gone, I didn't think I had anything left."

"That had to have been very difficult for you." She set down her fork, her empathy and understanding as tangible as the brush of her hand on his. "Only a truly good man would have done something like that."

"I don't know about good. It was the right thing." He let her touch comfort him, just a little, all he could allow, and twined his fingers through hers. It felt good to hold on to someone. He'd been alone for an excruciatingly long time. "My kids were able to come to terms with Lainie's abandonment. They made their peace with her. That was worth any wound to me."

Her hold on him tightened, telling him she understood. She saw the man he was, for better or worse, scars and all, and she didn't think less of him. She had scars of her own, too.

They were like souls, after all.

Tucker yanked open the dryer door and dug out the warm mound of clothes. They tumbled into the basket at his feet as the television droned from the living room down the hall. His cousin had taken over the couch and found a movie on the satellite.

He liked Sean, but he wasn't in the mood for a movie or company. Being trampled by a raging bronc had not been nearly as painful as Sierra admitting she didn't love him.

Enough. That was the word she'd used. What did that mean? And why had she cut things off between them? He fished the last sock out of the depths of the dryer, tossed it into the basket and straightened.

Just like that. He had thought she would have been comforted by his land purchase. A guy looking for fun, one who easily bolted, didn't make a cash land purchase large enough to terrify a lesser man. He'd laid his heart on the table. He'd risked showing her the man he was and it hadn't swayed her. She had looked at him and had seen someone who could abandon her.

Agony wrenched through him. He opened the washer and hauled the load of jeans into the dryer. When he'd been injured, he had gritted his teeth and gutted out his recovery without painkillers and faced rather painful therapy without balking. He was tough. In his work, he was banged up pretty hard on a daily basis. But the extreme torture seizing him now was purely emotional and yet it hurt worse than all the rest. He could barely breathe.

What had he been thinking getting serious with a woman? He cleaned out the lint trap. Crazy, maybe. That had to be the only explanation. This involved, committed, shattered heart thing was for the birds. He spun the dial and the dryer chugged to life. He swung the basket off the floor, grimly determined to forget his terrible mistake and never get involved again. Lesson learned. He would never let another woman anywhere close to his heart.

Every step he took made the agony worse. He shouldered down the hallway, frustrated, trying to hide the fact he felt as if he were bleeding to death. Just forget her, Tucker. Let her go.

The back door swung open, a man's voice mumbled low and a woman's answered with an amused chuckle. Autumn tumbled through the threshold, her hand entwined with her fiancé's. Ford Sherman towered in the doorway, clearly besotted, as he reluctantly said good-night. Autumn went up on tiptoe to kiss him—time to exit stage right—and it took all of Tucker's self-discipline not to remember kissing Sierra on that porch with the starlight falling over them like grace. He hiked up the stairs as fast as he could go. He retreated to his room and began folding clothes and packing them into his suitcase.

Don't think about her. He was a goal-oriented man. He could banish her if he put his mind to it. The trouble was that she was in his heart, in every part of it, and that wasn't something he could budge. Frustrated, he paired up his socks, working methodically. Maybe putting distance between him and this town would help. After all, his land deal would take time to close and he didn't have anything better to do than to get back to work.

Downstairs, the back door opened and he

focused on the familiar sound of Frank kicking off his boots and dropping his keys.

"Dad! How did the big date go?" Autumn's voice sailed up the staircase, full of happy hope. "Did you and Cady have a nice time?"

"Passable." Humor layered that word, saying more than Dad would probably like. "Not that I'm going to tell you about it, little girl."

"Ooh, it did go well." Autumn was a huge fan of Cady's. Cady had been taking riding lessons from Autumn since last summer, and they had gotten close. "So, will there be a date number two?"

"She said yes when I asked her, so I guess so." Dad sounded happy. Happier than he'd been since Tucker could remember.

Lord, if Cady makes him this happy, then please work this out well for the two of them. He plucked a T-shirt out of the basket and gave it a snap. Sometimes love worked. He liked Cady. She definitely was kind enough to love Dad the way he deserved.

The way Sierra apparently couldn't do for him. His guts seized tighter, adding to his general misery. He hadn't figured she would reject him. He'd thought she felt the same way he did, wrapped up in love and devotion, his heart taking him on an adventure he'd never been on before.

"Sean! Did you get settled in okay?" Dad sure sounded chipper. Sean's answer came as an indistinguishable mumble, one Frank chuckled at. "Good. That movie looks interesting. I'll be down to finish watching it with you. Got to check on my son."

At least he had warning, Tucker thought, as he folded the shirt and packed it. Every beat of his father's step made the inevitability closer. It was time to leave. Normally he was eager to go. He kept distance between him and everyone else with good humor and a solid exit plan. But it wasn't working this time. He felt heavy and conflicted as he shook the wrinkles out of another shirt and folded it. What was different?

"What's going on?" Frank filled the

doorway, loosening his tie. "Looks like you're packing."

"Time to go. I got the okay from the doc, so it's back to work." He ignored the hitch of sorrow and shook another shirt out of the basket. Bull riding didn't interest him like it used to do. It didn't take a genius to know why. "I've been hanging around here too long."

"Getting tired of us?"

"You know it." He set his jaw. He had to keep things light. That was the way to handle this. He folded the tee in thirds and dropped it onto the stack.

"I figured you might stay this time." Dad ambled in, pausing, his silence heavy with understanding. After a few minutes, he spoke again. "What about Sierra Baker?"

"What about her?" A pair of jeans were left at the bottom of the basket so he shook those out.

"You and she were getting close. I thought—" He didn't finish. He didn't have to.

Tucker knew what everyone thought. "You weren't wrong."

"What happened?"

He ignored the tug of emotion his father's caring caused. He shoved aside the need to let anyone close. It hurt too much. "Nothing that a little distance can't fix."

"Hmm." Frank seemed to think about that, but he didn't walk away. Understanding set across his features. He must already know what had happened. "I met Green on the road. He was driving to town, I was coming home. We rolled down our windows and chatted for a few."

"Nothing new about that." He laid the jeans into place and opened his top dresser drawer. Since he knew what was coming, he braced himself and prepared for the subject he'd trade his retirement account not to talk about.

"Green said he accepted an offer on his place. Your offer. The sale closes in a few weeks." He didn't sound surprised or angry his son hadn't shared a big decision like that with him. "I take it Sierra knows about it?"

"She knows." More clipped than he meant to sound and he winced. Too late to take the tone back, so he dug a half dozen pairs of socks out of his drawer and dumped them into the suitcase. "I don't want to talk about it."

"Sure, I get that." Easygoing, that was Dad, and persistent. He crossed his arms over his chest, watching the packing process curiously. "I can sympathize with Sierra."

"Sheesh, thanks, Dad." He rolled his eyes and opened another drawer.

"I meant I had a spouse run out on me. I can guess how she might be feeling." Frank Granger was still ten feet tall, still kind as could be, and always knew just what to say. "It does something to you when a marriage ends like that. When you've put your all into it only to find out the reason it wasn't working was because the other person was just going through the motions. Your mom took off to find what made her happy, since it wasn't ever going to be me, and left me with the responsibilities. All of them."

"I hear what you're saying." Tucker could picture Sierra sitting across the booth from him in the diner, and felt the regret as she'd turned him down for good. "None of it makes me feel any better."

"Do you love this girl?"

"I do." It panicked him, it calmed him, it made him crazy all at once. All he wanted was her. She hadn't been in his plans, but it felt as if he'd just been wandering until she'd lassoed his heart. He sorted through his T-shirts, decided which to take and which to leave but he couldn't concentrate. "She doesn't want to be anything more than friends."

"I don't believe that for a second. I've seen the way that girl looks at you."

"She said love isn't enough."

"Sometimes it's not."

That was the simple truth he feared. Tucker

shut the lid and zipped the case closed. Time to get out of Dodge. An escape plan was the only strategy he had. He couldn't stay here where he would bump into Sierra in town. That would rip him apart more.

"Want help packing?" his dad asked.

"No, go on downstairs and put your feet up. Take it easy. You have to be wrung out after your first date in over thirty years." A little good-natured kidding always helped lighten the mood and chase away feelings he didn't want to deal with.

"I *am* a little worse for the wear. If you're sure?"

"Yep. I've got it covered." He liked seeing his dad relaxed and happy and hopeful. "Does this mean we'll be getting a new stepmom?"

"Don't get the cart before the horse, son." Frank chuckled, but his flush turned a deep, telltale red.

Dad married again? That was something to look forward to. Tucker turned to his closet so his father couldn't see him grin.

* * *

I'm late, late, late. Sierra squinted through the wet dotting the windshield between wiper swipes. The country road ahead of her was a smear of concrete and painted lines bordered by smatterings of fallow bunchgrass. What the rain wasn't blurring, her tired eyes did for her. She hadn't gotten more than a few winks of sleep last night, tossing and turning with Tucker Granger on her mind.

He was still there front and center with his purchase and sale agreement for the Green's ranch and his heart on his sleeve.

She'd done the right thing. She had to believe that. Her fingers tightened on the steering wheel until the plastic bit into her skin. She had Owen. She had responsibilities. She'd worked hard to right her son's world and to help him feel secure again. She couldn't trust her son's heart and her own to an uncertain future. She knew Tucker wasn't like Ricky. But knowing that didn't stop the panic from clutching her like a smash-and-grab thief. She had to be sensible regardless of how much it hurt.

What she should be thinking about was her new job. The inn's driveway came into sight just before the outskirts of town and she hit her signal. Something big and black rolled into her view in the oncoming lane. An RV, top of the line and impressive even in the rain. The wipers stroked at a tinted windshield, so she couldn't see who was driving. She didn't need to. She could tell by the wrench of sorrow behind her rib cage.

Tucker. Memories assaulted her as she slowed to take the driveway. His confident manliness as he'd approached her that day in the hospital, his kind comfort he'd given her son, his steady friendship when he'd sat beside her during the surgery. His consideration, his kiss, his flowers. His unending generosity and solid friendship with Owen. Tears burned in her throat as she spun the wheel blindly and came to a stop in the paved lane. The enormous RV blew by her, pulling a horse trailer, and she wondered if

Tucker had recognized her—of course he had—and if he felt as if a vital organ had been ripped out of his body, too.

Probably not. She took a slow breath, trying to blow out some of the pain. She gripped the wheel so tight, her knuckles were white. She pried her fingers open and sat for a moment, letting the wind buffet the side of the car and rain sluice down the windows. When she looked back, since January Tucker had paid so much attention to Owen. Maybe that's all this had ever been. Tucker wanting to settle down, wanting a son, wanting the next phase of his life.

See how right she'd been to turn him down? A man could come into their lives, stir things up and who knew what would happen then? Tucker had so many options in his life. It was hard to imagine he would be content staying settled.

Or, maybe that was simply her fear talking. It was safer to avoid the tough questions and pretend the real reasons all had to do with the man, not with her.

Whichever, it hardly mattered now. He was gone. Heading back to his exciting life. She was safe. Her son was safe. Life could get back to normal—*if* she could figure out how to fill the hole his leaving had carved into her soul. If she could find a way to rid him from her memories and from her thoughts, then she could go on as if nothing had happened.

It wasn't fair that one man could impact her this much. She straightened her shoulders, gathered her strength and took hold of the steering wheel. *Lord, I trust you to see me through to where I need to go.*

She didn't feel exactly alone as she gave the vehicle a little gas and meandered down the lane. The inn towered ahead, a beautiful structure with southern country charm and western touches. Her new job awaited and so did her life without Tucker Granger.

Chapter Fifteen

"I hear the Greens' sale closed. Tucker owns the property." Jeri Lynn sawed a knife through a peeled potato and pretended she didn't have an agenda.

Sierra was *so* not fooled. She grabbed a potato from the sink and the peeler from the counter. She hoped she adequately hid the hit of misery seizing her. She missed the man every day since he'd left town. "Tucker Granger. He's the only topic of conversation you can think of? You haven't asked me how my new job is going. We should talk about that."

"I'm glad Cady has been able to give you

more hours." Jeri Lynn's look of feigned in-nocence didn't fade. She had the attitude of a mom on a mission but at least she took the hint. For now. "Are you enjoying working for her?"

"Yes. It's a very pleasant working environment." The Lord had provided a part-time job, opening a window when a door had closed, and Sierra appreciated it very much. What could have been a precarious finan-cial position had worked out for the best. "There's a chance I can move to full time. The manager is happy with my work."

"Oh, that's wonderful." Jeri Lynn put down her peeler. The big country kitchen of the farmhouse framed her like a picture with white cabinets, cupboards, appliances and a long stretch of yellow counter.

Sierra thought of the countless meals she'd helped her mom prepare in this house over the years. It had been a nice place to grow up, filled with laughter and love during the good times and solace in the tougher times. Maybe it's why she'd wanted to stay for supper after work instead of taking Owen and rushing home. She desperately needed comfort. She missed Tucker. She had broken her own heart by refusing his love.

There she went, thinking of Tucker again. She winced and finished peeling the potato.

"Mom?" Owen wandered in with the stuffed Slayer tucked in the curve of his arm. "I'm hungry. Can I have another cookie?"

"Supper is an hour away, young man." She plunked the potato onto the cutting board and wiped her hands on her apron.

"Would you like some potato?" Jeri Lynn ran the knife through the russet and popped a small slice into her mouth. "It's not a cookie, but it will tide you over."

"I guess." Owen scampered over, his cowlick standing straight up, mussed from the Stetson he'd been wearing earlier, the one Tucker had given him.

"Has the rodeo started yet?" Jeri Lynn asked as she grabbed a cereal bowl and added a handful of slices to it. "I hear cheering in the living room."

"Yep. They're calf ropin' right now. But not Tucker. He rides Slayer tomorrow. He told me. He and I talk all the time. We're buddies."

"So I've heard," Jeri Lynn practically sang as she sprinkled a light layer of salt on the slices and handed over the bowl. She had never looked as happy. "I have a big question for you. How much does he talk to your mom?"

"Mother!" Really. Sierra dropped her peeler and gave Owen a light, loving nudge in the direction of the living room. "You don't want to miss the calf roping."

"No, cuz Calvin's going to be up real soon. He's Tucker's friend, too." Owen stopped in the archway, adorable, big blue eyes glittering with excitement. "I got to talk to him when Tucker called. They were having hamburgers on the barbecue."

"Nice." She tried not to wonder how easily

Tucker had gone back to his life without her. It wasn't as if she'd given him a choice, so why did it hurt so much?

Before her mother could grill the boy more, she escorted him into the next room. The living room was comfortable more than impressive, full of overstuffed furniture and antiques handed down through the family. Images of a horse and rider chasing down a running calf flashed across the wide-screen in the corner and Owen was instantly mesmerized. What a relief.

Maybe that would be the end of the Tucker talk. Fine—probably not, but a girl could hope. She was shattered enough and talking about him only stirred up the knowledge she could have made a different choice. But she'd been too scared of getting hurt again. Not too proud of herself, she sauntered into the kitchen recognizing that gleam in her mother's eyes. "Don't even go there, Mom."

"I can't help it. Don't think I don't know

what went on between you and Tucker."
Jeri Lynn shook her knife with motherly
emphasis before chopping up another
potato. "I heard all about the diner. He
declared his love for you and you turned
him down."

"I can't talk about this." It tore her apart.
She regretted ending their relationship—
friendship, she corrected. Except for his
kiss. Except for the flowers and his steady
courtship and his determination to build a
bond with her son. The backs of her eyes
burned and she blinked hard, refusing to
let her walls down. She was well fortified.
As long as she kept Tucker at a distance she
could not get hurt.

"A man doesn't buy a hundred thousand
acres if he isn't serious." In the other room,
the roar of the crowd crescendoed as the
rodeo continued. Apparently something very
exciting was going on. Jeri Lynn gathered
up the slices and spread them out in a casserole dish. "He bought that land for you and
Owen. The Greens have the most gorgeous

house, a nice place to raise a family. That man is letting you know he's ready to settle down."

"The way Ricky was?" She lowered her voice so Owen wouldn't accidentally overhear. "Tucker and I are worlds apart. I wish it wasn't that way, but it is. He went back to his life the minute the doctor gave him the okay. He was never going to stay."

"Maybe you broke his heart so he couldn't bear to hang around. Did you ever think of that?"

All the time. In the quiet of the night when she should be asleep. In the middle of her shift at the diner when someone from the Granger family came in for a meal. While reading Owen his bedtime story and remembering the cozy togetherness of the evening Tucker had spent with them. Agony surged through her with unbearable force. She plunked another peeled potato onto the cutting board. "Remember how I told you it takes a great man to be better than no man at all? Tucker's a good man, but that's it."

"Admit it. You love him." Jeri Lynn softened, a mother wanting her daughter to find happiness and so sure she was right. "You love him and it scares you."

"Fine, I admit it. But it's not like I'm going to marry him. Things are different this time around. I can't follow my heart. I need someone who will always be there, someone I can always count on. I have Owen." The agony inside her twisted harder. This could not go on. "Mom, I can't talk about this anymore. It hurts too much."

"So, you love him deeply. It's as I thought." Jeri Lynn's tone gentled. "Don't you worry. God will work this all out for the best. I have faith He will bring you together."

"Mom, this isn't helping." A strange sensation skidded down the back of her neck, slid down her spine and burrowed into her stomach. Almost as if something was wrong.

The topic of conversation was wrong, she

decided, and did something about it. She'd made her decision, Tucker had accepted it and there was no going back.

Regrets haunted her, but whatever they'd had was over. There was no sense debating the might-have-beens. She couldn't turn back time and remake her decision. If she could, would she have given Tucker a different answer? She might have. "How was your last Ladies Aid meeting?"

Jeri Lynn launched into an amusing tale as they peeled and sliced and whipped up a white sauce together. The painful tension behind Sierra's sternum eased as the minutes ticked away. She was setting the table when footsteps padded through the living room and into the kitchen. Her dad stood there in his barn clothes and asked over the blare of the calf roping in the next room, "Where's Owen?"

"Isn't he watching the rodeo?" Sierra slid the casserole into the oven.

"No. The TV is on, but no little boy. I

checked the bathroom. I checked upstairs. He's not in the barn, since I just came from there." He scratched the back of his head. "Where did he go?"

"Tomorrow's the big day," Tucker told his companion as he polished off the last of his roast beef sandwich. "I'm ready for it. I've missed the challenge. You know I like challenges."

A rustle came as his friend nodded in sympathy, red hair ruffling in the slight breeze wafting down the main aisle. The horse barn was busy with folks rushing to finish their work before hurrying off to grab a bite. The rodeo was done for the day. Tomorrow would be his first time in competition. He'd missed it, but coming back here wasn't the same. These days more than ever he was just passing time. It hurt to think about. He grabbed a carrot stick left over from his salad and gave it to his companion.

Jack accepted it, his velvety muzzle brushing Tucker's palm. Jack was a good listener and an incomparable friend.

"I miss her." That plain, sorry fact troubled him most. He'd never thought the day would come when he was this tangled up in knots over a woman. A woman he would do anything for, risk everything for and lay down his life to protect if he had to. He rubbed his sternum but the emotional hole remained. He shut the lid on the container before Jack could get hold of one of the leftover fries and stood. Clean straw tumbled off his jeans. "Thanks for the company, buddy. I'll go fetch my book and a cup of tea and be right back. Okay?"

Jack whinnied, big chocolate eyes holding a single question.

"Fine. I'll bring back a treat. How does an apple sound?"

Jack nickered in approval, fond of apples, and stomped his foot, nosing the gate as if to say, "Get a move on and hurry back with my treat."

Tucker rubbed the gelding's nose, the bond

of friendship deep between them. "All this time it's been you and me. We're family. There's nothing light and easy about that."

Jack lifted his chin and narrowed his eyes as if to say, "About time you figured it out."

"Right. I know, it took me long enough." With his hands on the horse's nose and his guard down, he could feel what Jack's friendship had taught him. The conversations that mattered most were the ones which came straight from the heart. "I love you, too, buddy. I'll be back with your apple."

He hadn't taken three steps down the aisle when his cell jangled. He recognized the number on the screen. "Hi, Dad. Are you at the airport?"

"Didn't make it there, son." The grim tone in his father's usual relaxed manner was warning enough. Something was wrong. "I've been tied up with search and rescue. I wanted to tell you before you see it on the news. There's an Amber Alert out for a missing child. Owen."

His knees buckled. He grabbed the wall for support, upsetting a territorial horse in the nearby stall who began neighing shrilly. Tucker slumped against the wood, trying to catch his breath. "It wasn't Ricky, was it? Owen wasn't taken, right?"

"We don't know for sure. He's simply missing. We don't know if he walked away or not." Dad sounded choked up. "I wanted you to hear it from me. I know you're close to the boy."

"Close?" That wasn't the word. He hadn't taken the time to figure it out, but the crash of abject fear hitting his chest like a tsunami was a clue. "Yeah, we're close. What can I do?"

"Nothing, from Tulsa. Hold on." Frank's voice was muffled, holding the phone to his chest, talking to someone else. There was the snap of grass beneath boots, the rattle of a bridle before his dad came back on the line. "Tucker? I've got to go. I'll keep in touch. Let you know what's going on."

"Where are you now?"

"Combing the fields around the Boltons' farmhouse." A horse blew out his breath. Dad must be on his gelding, Rogue. "It wouldn't hurt for you to call Sierra. She could use some support about now."

"She wouldn't want to hear from me." He could barely get the words out. His emotional pain could hurt worse than any physical trauma. He sucked in a shallow breath and pushed off the wall. "She and I aren't even friends, Dad."

"Seems to me you never were. You were always meant to be something more. Call her."

When he disconnected, Tucker stared at the phone for a full minute. Shock and terror were a strong combination. He thought of little Owen lost, alone, scared, maybe hurting, and it broke him to the quick. Sierra must be half-destroyed and frantic. She loved her son so much.

"Sorry, Jack." He bolted to the stall and grabbed his coat and keys. The big red gelding watched him with concern, knowing something was wrong. "It's Owen. I've got to help find him. I'll bring you that apple later."

The horse nibbled Tucker's hair, an old show of affection.

"You take care, too," he said, pushing through the gate. He had a lot to do—ask Calvin to look after Jack, scrub tomorrow's event and move mountains if that's what it took to get a seat on a plane home.

The overwhelming, soul-stealing panic would not abate. Sierra tightened her grip on the high-powered flashlight Sheriff Sherman had given her. Snowflakes hovered in the air, weightlessly dancing on the wind, not deigning to touch the ground, forerunners of the storm blowing in. Slow-moving clouds steadily blotted out the constellations one by one.

"It's already twenty-three degrees." Neighbor Jeremy Miller sidled up to the crowd gathering in the middle of the intersection of Mustang Lane and Deer Brook Road.

"It's supposed to get down to ten degrees tonight. The wind's picking up, so that means windchill."

She couldn't feel the cold. She couldn't feel anything as Frank Granger dismounted, gave his big, dark bay a pat and left the horse standing in the road alongside a dozen other horses and riders. "It's going to start snowing hard. I say we keep looking."

"We can't s-stop." Sierra sputtered, on the verge of hyperventilating. Frank had been the one to find Owen's sneaker print in the shoulder of the road a quarter mile down from her parents' house. "He's out here somewhere and he didn't take his coat."

"I won't stop searching." Frank's gloved hand settled on her shoulder, a dependable weight. Fatherly concern gentled the rugged planes of his face. "I swear to you, I will not stop until I find him."

What he didn't say, what none of the several dozen searchers on the ground and as many more on horseback wanted to admit, was that it was already dangerously cold for a little boy not dressed for the conditions. After six hours in the elements, Owen could be in serious trouble. She swallowed hard against the horror threatening to take her over. Owen had to be all right. She could not live with the thought of any other option.

"I won't stop either," the sheriff vowed. Ford Sherman had moved from Chicago in November and already he'd fit seamlessly into the community. He was a resolute, caring lawman who had gone to extremes to help her with Owen before. Ford cared, and it shone on his chiseled features as he studied the area map he'd anchored with a thermos and three rocks on the open tailgate of his four-wheel-drive. He aimed his flashlight at the areas searched and the meadows and roads still needing careful exploration.

"I'll take Autumn, Merritt, Hal Plum and Scotty." Frank tapped the map, and exchanged a silent look of understanding with the sheriff. "We'll do a thorough search here."

Of the river. Her strength left her and she stumbled against the side of the vehicle. A strong grip wrapped around her elbow, holding her up. Justin Granger, as impressive as his brother and father, loomed against the night sky, his Stetson speckled with snow. "Easy, there. Maybe you should take a break."

"I can't." How could she rest for even one nanosecond when she didn't know if Owen was all right, if he needed her, if he was freezing or hurt or crying?

"Let me take you home to your mom." Rori Granger waltzed up, compassion itself, and wrapped an arm around her.

Sierra shook her head. She couldn't stand the thought of giving up. She had to do everything she could to find him. Everything. "I just need something to do, so I don't have to think."

"Don't worry, gal." Frank had mounted up and swung his gelding around. "We'll find him. Keep the faith."

Yet he was leading the search along the

river for a second time. She feared she knew why. They suspected Owen had headed for the dangerously fast and mercilessly cold water, judging by the direction his sneaker track was pointing.

The darkness swallowed the riders as they trotted off, steeled shoes ringing on the pavement, echoing with a note of hopelessness she could not give in to. She'd prayed so many prayers for Owen since her dad had discovered him gone, but she figured one more plea wouldn't hurt. *Watch over him, Father. Please let him be okay. Please let him be found.*

Something icy brushed her cheek. Snow tumbled earnestly from a pitch-black sky. Headlights cut through the growing storm and rolled to a stop nearby. Cady Winslow and the inn's manager, Eloise, climbed out of an SUV, bundled well against the cold.

"We have warm beverages and hot sandwiches," Cady called as she opened her passenger door and hauled out a huge insulated carrier. "We thought the searchers might need some refueling."

"It's a cold night," Eloise added, carrying two large dispensers. "This will help keep everyone going."

"I will be okay now," Sierra said to Justin and Rori, who gently let her go. "I can't believe what everyone is doing for Owen."

"In a small town at times like this, we're all family." The sheriff stepped in to answer. "Sierra, I'll put you with the group walking the next field up the road. The mayor is in charge. Report to him, and make sure you get some coffee and something to eat, got it?"

She nodded numbly, aware of the sympathetic looks everyone gave her. She heard Ford's radio squawk and adrenaline pumped through her. Was it bad news? She didn't think she could stand to hear it but strained to listen.

"Good. At least we can rule out that field," Ford answered. "Bring your team in. We can get some food and coffee before I send you back out."

Relieved it wasn't bad news and upset

it wasn't good, she tightened her hold on her flashlight and stumbled forward. Cady pressed a paper cup into her hands. As if from a distance, the strong smell of sweetened coffee braced her, but she shook her head to refuse a sandwich. Her stomach lurched, one big, terrified knot.

"My team, time to go!" Tim Wisener called out as he unwrapped a sandwich. "We'll eat in the Jeep."

Snow mantled the mayor's four-wheel-drive, and Sierra found herself sitting in the backseat, unsure how she'd gotten there. The cup burned warmth through her insulated gloves and the fragrant steam bathed her face. As the other passengers settled in, doors closed and Tim started the engine, she sipped the coffee, washing the taste of fear off her tongue, but the teeth of it remained, sinking deep into her soul.

The snow fell harder, obscuring the vehicles pulling up and driving away full of townspeople determined to help. Another band of horses and riders plodded by, heads bowed against the rising wind. She could not stand to think what would happen if they could not find him. She did not think she could stand to lose Owen.

A pickup rolled to a stop next to the sheriff's Jeep. Sierra caught sight of the man bounding down from the driver's seat and her pulse flatlined. Not the darkest night or the heaviest snow could disguise from her the dependable strength of his shoulders or the confident swagger as Tucker Granger strolled into the fall of the battery-powered lantern light.

He'd come back. She could not believe her eyes. She blinked, but he remained a dark silhouette that the storm could not diminish. As if he sensed her scrutiny, his blue gaze found hers with unerring precision. The weeks of separation, of regret and bereavement, vanished as if they'd never occurred. There was only the leap of emotional connection between them, a bond that would not break. The Jeep took off and carried her away and still the connection remained, her one comfort on a hopeless night.

Chapter Sixteen

The snow erased any chance of finding a shoe print or any clue the boy had passed this way. Frustrated, more scared than he'd ever been in his life, Tucker did not take his eyes from the ground as he swept the high-powered flashlight on the pristine snowfall in front of him. The line of folks who walked nearly shoulder to shoulder with him through the fallow cornfield shouted out Owen's name in intervals.

No answer. No sign of the kid. All evening through and most of the night had been one long, desperate prayer. *Please. Please keep him safe. Please let us find him. Please let him be okay.*

Tucker knocked the snow off his hat and kept going. All through his frantic search to find a way home—one of the rodeo promoters had offered her company jet—the flight to Wyoming and the snowy drive from the airport, one thing had eaten at the back of his mind. Why had the boy left?

Owen was a polite little guy, so it was hard to imagine him leaving his grandparents' house without telling his mom. Sierra kept a good eye on the boy. Why had he slipped away and where would he want to go?

The kid had friends in town. Ford had half the searchers combing the land and roadways heading to Wild Horse, thinking maybe Owen had set off for home or to see someone he knew. Owen did like animals. The Greens' ranch wasn't far from here— Tucker's place now. Would the little guy have wanted to see Cotton Ball?

A gust of below-freezing wind sliced neatly through his winter wear and he resisted the urge to shiver. He hauled out his cell, squinted at the screen to make sure he had a signal—he saw one bar—and punched in Mr. Green's number. He'd agreed to lease the main house back to the older couple for a spell to give them plenty of time to find a new home, pack and move. He listened to ring after ring, realizing Mr. Green was probably out here somewhere helping with the search, but maybe Mrs. Green—

"Hello?" A wobbly voice answered in a rush. After Tucker explained his concern, Mrs. Green offered to make sure Cotton Ball was alone. After fifteen long, anxious minutes his cell rang with the news there was no sign of the little boy, and she'd checked the barn and the horse stable, too.

The horse stable. Owen might not have realized Tucker had taken Jack with him when he'd left. What if the boy had gone to see his favorite horse? The back of his neck tingled, the way it did when he was sure heaven was watching. The walk from Owen's grandparents' house was a few miles—a long way for the tyke, but doable. He could have walked right down the country road, which would explain why he hadn't left more than a single shoe print. Traffic was haphazard on Mustang Lane since it wove through ranching country, which explained why no one had spotted the boy.

"Hey, Chip." He shouted to be heard down the line. "I've got to check something."

"Go ahead." Owen's grandfather paused for a moment. "Do you know where he might be?"

"I'll let you know." He took off at a run, sweeping the flashlight's beam at the uneven terrain in front of him. Thick snow gripped his boots trying to slow him down, but he kept going. The instant he dropped into the shelter of his truck, he turned the keys and dialed the ranch. No answer in the house, the barns or in the foreman's cottage. Dad must have pulled everyone for the search.

Mustang Lane was one long battle of poor visibility and blowing snow, but he gritted his teeth and went on his instinct and rote memory. He'd driven the country road more times than he could count. He kept his eyes peeled for the shadow of a child on the road, although he doubted he would find Owen out in the open. He charged up the driveway, cloaked with snow, frustrated by the slow going. He hopped out to open the cow gate at the side of the garage and left it open, barreling up the service road to the barns. Because of the weather, no animals ran up to the fence to greet him. When he climbed out of the truck in front of the south stable, the eerie silence wrapped around him.

"Owen?" His voice reverberated down the main aisle, carried on the bitter wind. The warmth of the snug stable embraced him with the comforting scents of hay, alfalfa and horse, but nothing could drive away the fierce, intense need to find the boy, to protect him, to make sure he was safe. It was a need unlike any he'd ever felt before, one that had no measure and no end.

Horses started, coming up to their gates to whinny greetings or requests for attention.

He marched passed them, eating up the distance to Jack's end stall. "Owen, are you here?"

No answer. The animals were calm, not agitated by anything different in the building. He kept running, but inside his hopes slumped. The boy wasn't here.

A white-faced Hereford poked her velvety nose over her stall and mooed. Wanting attention, no doubt. Buttercup's ears were up and her chocolate eyes bright as a puppy's as she did a little dance against her gate. The cow mooed again with clear excitement and glanced down the long stretch of stalls. She mooed a third time.

Buttercup liked children. Tucker kept running, not daring to hope but his hope rose anyway. Jack's stall was ajar, and Tucker skidded to a stop. Tears burned behind his eyes at the sight of a little, tousle-haired boy curled up in the clean straw, a riding blanket from the tack room draped over him.

"Tucker?" Owen sat up, teeth chattering. His rodeo T-shirt, the one Tucker had given him that day in the hospital, was wet through. He frowned, puzzled. "You're not supposed to be here."

"Sure I am." He pushed aside the gate and strolled into the stall. "If you need me, then I'm here."

"You gotta ride Slayer in the rodeo." Owen rubbed his eyes, smearing a single tear. "You gotta go back."

"It's just one ride and it's not nearly as important as you and your mom." He knelt down to get a better look at the boy. Pale, trembling, a bit blue around the lips. "You must be pretty cold from walking all this way in the snow."

"A little." Owen's chin went up, a determined little man.

"Your mom's pretty worried." Tucker unzipped his coat. "She didn't know what happened to you."

"I left." Misery twisted his button face. "I love my mom."

"I know." He tugged away the damp blanket, wet from the boy's clothes. He took one look at the jeans and sneakers. Sure enough, the boy was soaked clear through. "I love your mom, too."

"She works two jobs so I can have food and the mortgage payment. That's really hard."

Someone had apparently listened in on an adult conversation. Tucker knew about that, since he'd done the same thing at that age. He gathered the boy into his arms and held him against his chest, offering his body heat. "I don't think your mom minds. She loves you, Owen. That's what love is. You put those you love first, ahead of yourself."

"That's why I'm gonna live in Jack's stall." Owen's arms wrapped around Tucker's neck and held tight.

Nothing in the world had ever felt as sweet. Tucker held on hard, too, letting the deep feelings of affection and fatherly devotion take root in his soul. He loved this boy like his own son. "That's a good plan. It's comfortable here and warm enough for a horse, but not for a little boy."

"I know." His teeth chattered loudly, the boy a dear weight in Tucker's arms. Owen sniffled. "But I'm not in the way."

"In whose way?" He couldn't imagine where the child had gotten that idea. Sierra's commitment to her son knew no bounds.

"That's why Daddy left. It was my fault." Owen shuddered, muffling a sob. "I heard Mom. Now she can't have a heart because of me. But I fixed it. I'm not in the way. Not anymore. You can marry my mom now."

An arrow straight to his chest. He wrapped his arms tighter around the child, knowing well the pain of being abandoned and the damage it did. You learned to keep a safe distance between yourself and others, keep it light and on the surface, to let nothing and no one in so deep that they would tear out a piece of you when they left. Because when someone you loved decided to stop loving you, it was hard to believe anyone else could truly love you enough to stay.

Tucker leaned his jaw against the crown of the boy's head, seeing the purpose of his life and the fork in the road. He loved Sierra. He'd always loved her but he had to make her believe it. His commitment deepened. Time to put both feet in. He would dust off the heart she'd broken, stand up and show her and Owen what a man staying looked like.

He maneuvered his cell out of his coat pocket. "Let's give your mom a call, okay?"

"Okay," Owen sniffled, as he burrowed harder against Tucker's chest and held on tight.

The night's bitter cold had crept into her bones and lingered. Sierra shivered, buttoned her hand-knit cardigan and thanked the emergency room doctor in the neighboring town of Sunshine. Now that the ordeal was over and Owen had been declared fine by the emergency room doctor, she felt the weight of her exhaustion. What she had to do was to get Owen home, a nice hot meal in them both and then straight to bed. She might be able to grab a few hours of sleep and start her shift a little late at the diner.

Owen, tired too, rubbed his eyes as he tripped down the wide, sterile hallway. "Mom, where's Tucker?"

"Waiting for us." Her stomach fluttered with anticipation. She was eager to be with the man who had found her child, the man who had moved mountains when Owen needed him—when she'd needed him. When her phone had rung in the middle of the Parnells' snowy cow pasture and Tucker's rich baritone had filled her ear, she'd cried with relief. Her son was safe and Tucker had found him. Tucker. She thanked God for him.

"Tucker!" Owen ripped away from her, his sneakers slapping against the tile floor, and ran straight to Tucker. The big man wrapped the boy against his chest, affection plain on his rugged face. As he stood with her son in his sheltering arms, she lost the last battle to keep her heart safe.

"How are you doing, buddy?" Tucker's

voice boomed across the waiting room, nearly drowned out by the sound of the legion of family hopping to their feet and charging across the nearly empty waiting room.

"Hand over that boy and let me get a look at him." Her dad fought to look relaxed and easygoing, but the strain and remnants of terror remained in his gray eyes. The fright faded away a bit more as he took Owen from Tucker.

Relief filled the room as the extended family circled the boy. Sierra recognized her sister-in-law Terri and her husband, Tom Gold, her in-laws Betty and Chip Baker and their son Boze, along with her five siblings and their families. Her mom crowded into the center to kiss Owen's cheek. Sierra's eyes blurred at the sight of the Grangers— including Mrs. Gunderson and Scotty, the ranch foreman—all stepping close to exchange words with Owen.

"Looks like there is going to be a happy ending." Tucker circled around the edge of the crowd and into sight, a man tall and dependable enough to fulfill her every dream. Dreams she'd lost surged to life, buoyant with hope. She was out of excuses, she was out of reasons why she couldn't risk her heart. He towered over her, a man great in her estimation, her one true love.

"A happy ending?" she quipped. She straightened her shoulders. She would not be afraid this time. She would take the risk and believe. "Maybe for Owen and me, but what about you? Your return to bull riding isn't off to a good start."

"Bull riding isn't my life. It never has been. You are." His dreamy blue eyes brightened with infinite tenderness. When he laid the palm of his hand against her cheek, she felt the strength of his love without end and his boundless devotion. He'd never been more serious before. "Don't make me go back to the rodeo. Marry me."

"Marry you?" Everything within her stilled. She should be terrified. She should be gathering up at least one hundred reasons why that would be an outrageous mistake, why she should stay safe, stay alone and not take a risk. Not a single reason flitted into her dazed mind. There was only the truth. She loved this man and his easy humor and kindness and commitment to her son. She realized Tucker had been showing her his heart all along. It was time to show him hers. "Yes, I would love to marry you."

"That's a relief. I was sure you were going to shoot me down again."

"It was tempting, but I missed you. Just a tiny bit."

"Only a *tiny* bit?"

"Fine, maybe it's slightly more than tiny." Her gray eyes lightened, a sure sign of happiness. She leaned into his touch, captivating. "Massively. Colossally. Infinitely."

"Without end. That's how I felt missing you." He moved in, sure of his course. Sure of this road he'd chosen. His real life was here on a ranch with his family, in the countryside he'd grown up in and with the people who'd made him the man he was.

His future was with Sierra, providing for her, protecting her, doing his best to make her the happiest woman on this earth. He'd found his heart, and it was her. "Your love is all I need for the rest of my life. I love you, Sierra."

"I love you." Tenderness polished her, making her lovelier than ever. No doubt shadowed her eyes, no fear, no sorrow. She laid her hand lightly on his chest, directly above his heart. "I love you so very much."

"I'm so glad to hear that." Honesty rang in his words. "I promise you this. I'll do my utmost never to let you down."

"I believe that. I believe in you." The wounds of her past were gone. Tucker had healed them. Tucker and his unyielding love, his stalwart commitment and the strength of his kindness. "I am going to love you forever."

"That's all? Not forever and a day?" A twinkle of humor hooked the corners of his hard-cut mouth. "Because that's how long I will love you."

She could not ask for more. She had true love. It was easy to see her future with Tucker, living next door to the Granger ranch. There would be horses to ride, muttons for Owen to bust and a lifetime of happiness because of the heart she felt beating next to her own. Because of the man who leaned in and kissed her with exquisite tenderness.

The moment froze, time slowed to a halt and the world disappeared. There was only their kiss. Flawless. Pure. Gently felt all the way to the soul. When Tucker lifted his lips from hers, the connection of their hearts remained. Yes, their future together was going to be a good one and she was grateful to the Lord for such a rare and precious blessing.

Outside the windows, night shadows faded. The sun chose that moment to dawn, gilding the world with a heavenly golden light. As Sierra tucked her hand in Tucker's much larger one and welcomed her son into her arms, she was sure the shadows in her life were behind her. It was the start of a glorious new day.

* * * * *

Dear Reader,

Welcome back to Wild Horse, Wyoming. I hope you have enjoyed the continuing stories of THE GRANGER FAMILY RANCH as much as I've enjoyed writing them. This time carefree, always-on-the-go cowboy Tucker Granger takes center stage. He's home recovering from a serious fall off a bareback bronc and becomes an ill boy's charity wish. Visiting little Owen Baker and his mom, Sierra, touches Tucker, and he can no longer say he's the same man. His fall and the near death experience that went with it have changed him. Sierra has been abandoned by her former husband, a man who was carefree and easygoing, too. What are the chances that God can lead the two of them down the road to happily-ever-after?

In these pages, I hope you find familiar faces in the returning characters that people the town of Wild Horse, Wyoming, and that you enjoy your glimpse into the ranching life and the wonder and rewards to be found there. I hope you fall in love along with Frank and Cady and are reminded that it is never too late for second chances. Most of all, I hope this story touches your heart, where it has touched me.

Thank you for choosing *His Country Girl*.

As always, wishing you the best of God's blessing,

Jillian Hart

QUESTIONS FOR DISCUSSION

1. What are Sierra's initial opinions of Tucker Granger? What does this say about her character? About her fears?

2. What is Tucker's reaction when he first sees Sierra in the hospital waiting room? How does he describe her? What does this tell you about his character? How do you know he's a good man?

3. Were you surprised when Tucker comes to stay with Sierra during Owen's surgery? Why do you think he does this? How does this change Sierra's opinion of him?

4. How did Tucker's accident affect him? What did he learn?

5. Family, friends and the town speculate about Sierra and Tucker's relationship. What part do they play in the budding romance? How does this affect Sierra? Tucker?

6. Sierra feels she cannot risk her son's heart. But what are her fears for herself?

7. Tucker is afraid he's falling in love with Sierra, but what does he do with that fear? How does he face it? What does that say about him?

8. What moral values do you think are important in this book?

9. Little Owen wants to be a professional rodeo rider so his real father will want to come see him. What impact does Owen's desire have on the story? On the romance? What does Owen learn?

10. What do you think are the central themes in this book? How do they develop? What meanings do you find in them?

11. In the beginning of the story, Sierra wrestles with the aftermath of her former husband's abandonment. She is afraid to trust in love again. How does she overcome this? What does Tucker actively do through the course of the book to gain her trust?

12. How does God guide both Sierra and Tucker? How is this evident? What do they learn about their faith?

13. What role do the animals play in the story?

14. Cady Winslow believes romance has passed her by, although she is secretly in love with Frank. What meanings do

you find in her story? Have you ever had a second chance in your life? How have you handled it?

15. What does Sierra learn about true love?